Godsend

RICH BOTTLES JR.

Godsend
By **Rich Bottles Jr.**

Burning Bulb Publishing
P.O. Box 4721
Bridgeport, WV 26330-4721
United States of America
www.BurningBulbPublishing.com

Cover designed by Gary Lee Vincent and Rich Bottles Jr.

First Edition.

Paperback Edition ISBN: 978-1-948278-31-7

Printed in the United States of America

Good Girls Just Want to be Bad

Rose Tuttle, the preacher's daughter, has been secretly rebelling against her father's tyranny for months. Disguised she takes a job singing in the saloon. When her father announces he's found her a husband, she rebels. That night, at the end of her performance, she removes her disguise. Now with no other choice, she becomes the newest member of the bad girls club.

Son of a Railroad tycoon, Hayden Lee has been going to hear a mysterious singer in the saloon for months. Her angelic voice reaches deep inside him and touches his soul. But he isn't prepared when he learns her identity as the preacher's daughter.

Unable to resist her, he longs to make her his. But there is no way, his father will accept a saloon singer for his wife. A woman from the bad girls club. Who will win, family or love? Or…Can he have both?

Bad Girls of the West
Scandalous Sadie
Ravenous Rose
Tempting Tessa
Nellie's Redemption

Want to learn about my new releases before anyone else? Sign up for my New Book Alert and receive a complimentary book.

Bad Girls of the West
Scandalous Sadie
Ravenous Rose
Tempting Tessa
Nellie's Redemption

Want to learn about my new releases before anyone else? Sign up for new book alert at http://www.sylviamcdaniel. com/sign-up-for-my-newsletter/ and receive a complimentary book.

CHAPTER 1

*R*ose Tuttle, the preacher's daughter, ran through the darkened streets of Fort Worth toward Hell's Half Acre. Fear filled her as she hurried down the back alleys, knife in hand.

Clenching the weapon in her fingers, she knew that no one would stand a chance against her at the moment.

Tonight, she had been planning to attend the Cattleman's Ball with her parents, but then her father introduced her husband-to-be to her.

A gangly, ugly man who was a preacher in a small town three hours west of Fort Worth. A man who looked at her with such lecherous desire in his eyes that he frightened her. Chilling was the only way to describe the carnal glee radiating from him.

Even the men in the saloon didn't gaze at her that way. They looked at her with adoring eyes, but this man glowered at her, like he couldn't wait to strip her down and do evil things to her body.

When she voiced her objections, her father had taken her

aside and told her she would marry this man tomorrow. That her time of searching for a godly man was over. He had found her one. Her rebellion was at an end.

All she could think was that she had to get away. She excused herself, snuck into another room, opened a window, and crawled out.

Now she was escaping to the White Elephant Saloon, her safe haven. The place where she could pretend her life was not the disastrous mess she hated. Her one escape.

Reaching the back of the saloon, she pulled open the door and entered. The stage manager glanced at her.

"I thought you were going to the Cattleman's Ball tonight," Randal said. He was the only one who knew who she really was and approved of her disguise.

"No, I'm not going to the ball. Where's my costume?"

"Are you all right?"

"No, I'm terrified. My father has found me a groom. We are to be wed tomorrow."

The man's eyes widened and he handed her the outfit she normally wore. A demure dress for a woman in a saloon with lace ruffles at the bottom and a low cut bodice that she had added more lace to hide the swells of her breasts. She went into the curtained off area and quickly changed.

"I'm not marrying him. He terrifies me." Her shoulders hunched as a shiver ripped through her body.

"Calm down, Rose. Take a deep breath. We'll figure something out."

"He's a preacher. I don't want to be a preacher's wife. I've seen how my father's congregation treats my mother and I will not be subjugated by my husband or his people."

She tossed her dress aside and pinned her tiny reticule inside her stage outfit. It contained all her cash and she feared

2

she was going to need that money in the coming days—everything she'd earned the months of singing here.

The many months of sneaking out to do what she loved.

When she stepped out, he helped her with her hat and the thick veil that covered her face. She could barely see through the tightly woven lace.

"Are you ready?"

Taking a deep breath, she grinned at him. "I'm ready. This is what I love. This is where I belong."

As soon as she said the words, it hit her. All she had to do was rip the veil off and let the men see who she was. That would ruin her. She would no longer be a woman a preacher would want to marry.

She would be a bad girl.

It seemed the perfect solution, but could she do it? What if the audience only loved her because of her mysteriousness?

Then not only would she be ruined, but she'd have no way to make a living.

Randal led her up the stairs to the stage and then he left her waiting in the shadows. The piano player was banging out music, which abruptly came to a halt.

"Ladies and gentlemen, we have a special surprise tonight. Mystery Flower was not supposed to appear, but she's here and she can't wait to sing for you. Please welcome, Mystery Flower."

An energy that excited Rose every time she sang spiraled through her when she came out on stage.

"Good evening," she said, excitement filling her. "Tonight, I was supposed to attend the Cattleman's Ball, but who wants to be with a crowd of boring socialites? Instead, I decided to be with you."

The crowd went wild with cheering and clapping.

Then she saw him sitting at his usual table, a drink in his hand as he stared at her. There was something about the man that always gave her a little thrill. Just staring into his eyes, a warmth would overcome her.

For months, he had attended her shows, sitting in the back, never approaching her. Always watching.

Her breath seemed to catch in her throat and she leaned her head back and began to belt out a song that she loved. The men raised their drinks in the air, cheering for her.

This was where she belonged. This was what she wanted to do. Sing. And her voice was a gift from God, to bring the people joy.

As the night wore on, she belted out song after song, the audience yelling, clapping and even singing along.

On the last song of the night, she began a ballad that everyone knew. The men, most of them quite drunk, sang along with her. And when she reached up and began to unwrap her disguise, they all stopped and stared.

Piece by piece, she removed the veil and finally the hat. She stood in front of them, holding out the last note of the ballad in her natural glory. Her face revealed.

The preacher's daughter had been exposed. No longer would she be anonymous.

When she finished, they all clapped and stomped their feet and a few even fired their guns off at the ceiling.

"Rose, Rose, Rose," they screamed.

"Good night, gentlemen," she called.

After she walked off the stage, she went back to the dressing room and changed her clothes. It was over, she was ruined. She wasn't even sure they would allow her to sing in the saloon again.

Now, the preacher man would no longer want her, but what would she do?

When she walked out of her dressing room, the man who sat at the table watching her every night was waiting.

His hands reached for her face and he pulled her to him and she watched in awe as his lips came crashing down on hers. Rose had never been kissed before and the way his mouth seemed to control hers, she didn't know what to think except that a heat begin to build inside her and she didn't want him to stop.

She didn't even know his name. Her hands came up between them and she pushed him away. The most sparkling blue eyes gazed at her and she wanted to lose herself in them. Sandy brown hair came to a peak on his forehead with his hair combed straight back. A straight nose, narrow jaw, small lips with dimples in his chin made her smile. But most of all...that kiss.

"What are you doing?"

"Rose Tuttle," he said, ignoring her question. "For months, I've wanted to kiss you."

"You shouldn't be back here," she answered.

"I gave the bouncer a gold coin. May I escort you home?"

That was such a tempting offer. It was a long walk to Sadie's home. She risked her father finding and taking her back to marry that horrible man. Maybe she should accept his kind offer.

"No, but you may accompany me to my friend's house. You see, I'm not returning home ever again."

He gazed at her steadily. "When you removed your disguise and the men told me who you were, I knew there had to be more to this story. Allow me to take you to your friend's home, and on the way, you can tell me what happened."

There was something about this man that made her think she should know him. But she didn't. And yet, he watched her every night for months. Applauded her, cheered her, and she felt a connection to him.

"I'm sorry, but I don't know your name," she said.

He bowed his head to her. "Hayden Lee. I have a business proposition to discuss with you."

She frowned at him. What could the man want with her? "And what would that be?"

"I'd like for you to become my mistress."

CHAPTER 2

*A*s soon as the words were out of his mouth, he knew they were the wrong thing to say. In horror, he watched as her mouth dropped open and the blood drained from her face.

While he doubted that she was an innocent, she was the preacher's daughter. And Reverend Tuttle liked to keep a tight rein on not only his congregation, but his family as well. In fact, Hayden was shocked at how the man didn't know of her performance here.

But after tonight, her secret was no more. Even now, he was certain someone was telling the reverend where his daughter was.

On the balls of her feet, she whirled around and walked out the door, leaving him standing in the backstage area alone. Rushing after her, he ran out into the darkened alley-way. When he caught up with her, he could see she was beyond angry.

Music played in the background and some cowboys were

outside hanging onto one another as they stumbled along, singing to the music.

Not looking at him, she continued to hurry.

"Every night, I have watched you sitting back at that table, wondering about you," she said. "Dreaming about you and making stories up in my head about who you were. And now, tonight, I don't want to know anything else about you. You're just as bad as some of the men in the saloon. You think I'm going to just lie down and spread my legs for you."

The woman's long legs were moving at a stride that he found hard to keep up with. He had majorly messed things up. What led him to ask her before he had wooed her?

"And another thing," she continued, "no woman, whether she's a preacher's daughter or a regular everyday woman, wants a man to ask her to lie on her back for him. At least take her to dinner before you drop the news that you just want sex with her. And no, that doesn't mean I would consider being your mistress even after dinner. Tonight, my reputation was ruined. I don't need you to create even more damage."

He was all but running to keep up with her. For three months, he'd been watching her every night, fantasizing about who this angel with a voice could be, and in fewer than five minutes, he'd destroyed any chance he had with her.

They turned onto Main Street where the crowds were large. But Hayden kept on talking trying to convince her he didn't mean to offend her. But if not as his mistress, what was he offering?

"I'm sorry. But your voice, it reaches down inside me and mesmerizes me. Like you, I've been dreaming of you."

Two men burst from a saloon, their fists flailing at one another. She stopped and turned to him. "Thank you for the compliment. Until you said the word mistress--well, let's just say I'm not interested in your business proposition. I'm not a whore."

The fight was becoming a street brawl and he grabbed her by the arm. "Let's get out of here."

He pulled her into an alley. "What are you doing?"

"I'm trying to save us from that group of drunken cowboys."

Moving quickly, he realized they were close to his carriage. "Let me take you home."

"I'm not getting into any carriage so that you can take advantage of me."

"No, you'd rather that drunk mob back there take you?"

Shouts rang out and men came running down the alley toward them.

Gripping her hand, he tugged her into a run.

"Stop," one of the men yelled. "She's too pretty for just one man."

They ran faster. "All right," she said, "you've convinced me. But let me warn you, I carry a knife and I'm not afraid to use it."

"Well, good, we may need it if we don't reach my carriage."

Just then his driver, George, pulled the carriage around the corner, his pistol already out and ready to end this fight before it began.

Hayden all put pushed her inside the door, his hands on her derriere.

"Don't touch me," she cried.

He jumped inside and watched as his driver clicked to the horses, charging the men standing in their way. Startled, they jumped back to let the carriage through. One pulled his gun out and fired at them, putting a hole in the walls of the carriage.

Hayden shoved her head down to protect her while his driver raced through the crowd. When they slowed, Hayden knew they were safe.

That was a narrow escape.

"I'm sorry for touching you inappropriately, but we were running out of time."

He didn't dare sit next to her and had taken the bench across from her.

"Where do you want to go?"

"Sadie King's home," she said.

"You're friends with Sadie?" he asked, stunned. His best friend, Levi Griffin was in love with the woman and planned to propose this very night at the Cattleman's Ball. For a second, he wondered if his friend had managed to get through the quagmire of emotional entanglements keeping him from his lady.

"We've been friends for many years," she said, her hand clutching her reticule. "Why does your name sound so familiar?"

With a sigh, he knew he had to tell her. And yet part of him believed she was lying. Surely, she recognized his face from the papers. Surely, she realized that his family owned the largest railroad in Texas.

No one was that innocent. No one. Especially, not a saloon singer.

"My family owns the railroad here in this part of Texas," he told her, knowing that now she would suddenly change her mind and decide to become his woman. For some reason, he was tickled at her outrage of his statement and didn't want to see that change.

"That's nice," she said.

That's nice? That was all she could say about his family

being the wealthiest in this town. Speechless, he sat and watched her. In the darkness, he couldn't see her dark brown eyes, but her pointed chin and high cheekbones expressed a sassiness about her that he longed to explore. The taste of her lingered on his lips and he resisted the urge to entwine her dark hair between his fingers and bring her mouth to his. For months, he'd dreamed of kissing her and yet he feared if he got near her, she would give him a taste of the knife she kept in her reticule.

"Why are you not returning home?"

She gave a sarcastic laugh. "Because my father has chosen a husband for me. And tomorrow we are to wed."

A husband? She was about to get married?

"When did you meet him?"

"Earlier this evening," she said. "And no, he's not to my liking. This marriage is not something that I want."

If she just met him, why in the world were they rushing the wedding?

"But that seems so soon," he said. His own sisters were not to venture out with any man they didn't know. And marrying someone the day after you met them seemed ludicrous.

"You're telling me. My father believes he knows what is best for me. And the women in our church are to obey their husbands, their fathers, and any man who gives them an order. I'm not doing too well with their idea of obedience."

He chuckled at the way she lifted her chin in defiance. "What are you going to do?"

She sighed. "I don't know."

Just then the carriage pulled in front of the house. She glanced around.

"Just looking out to make certain that no wagons filled with good-meaning churchgoers are here to capture me."

"Let me escort you to the door," he said, feeling her nervousness.

"Are you prepared to fight for me?"

He grinned. "I've almost fought for you once tonight. I think I can do it again."

She grinned at him. "Too bad, you were such a disappointment tonight. Do you have sisters?"

"Yes," he said.

"How would you feel if a man asked them to be his mistress?"

The woman had just trapped him. "They'd be dead come morning."

The driver opened the door and she shuffled forward. As she stepped out, George took her arm. Hayden, thinking he could maybe appeal to her better self, said, "Christians don't believe in killing."

She laughed as Hayden came to stand beside her, glancing around the darkness. "Keep telling yourself that lie. With your dismissal, there would be one less sinner in the world. Especially someone who offers opportunities to be his mistress."

Before he could respond, the door to the house opened and a blonde woman stood there. "Get in here, before you're spotted. Your father has everyone in town looking for you."

Rose turned back and smiled at him. "Good night, Mr. Lee. Good luck on finding a mistress."

Damn, the woman was downright sassy.

CHAPTER 3

*F*ear gripped Rose as she stared at her friend Tessa. She knew that her father would eventually find his way to Sadie's home.

"Hurry," Tessa commanded.

Hayden stood by the carriage. "Again, I apologize for my earlier remarks," he said. "You're right. I'd be a dead man if you had a brother."

She grinned at him and walked toward the house. "I have a brother," she said, glancing over her shoulder, giving him a saucy grin.

In the darkness, she couldn't tell if the man had the decency to blush, but she hoped she put the fear of God in him.

Tessa grabbed her by the arm and yanked her in the house. "I've been so worried. Who is that man?"

"Hayden Lee," she said.

"The railroad tycoon?"

"I guess," she said, giving a little shrug, really not caring that he was a rich man.

"Why was he apologizing to you?"

Shaking her head, she laughed. "He asked me to be his mistress."

"What? Should I get my gun and go after him?"

That would put some fear in him, but then again, she hoped he realized the error of his words.

"No, I made it clear I was not going to be any man's plaything."

Tessa shook her head. "Men! You would think they'd learn that a good woman is not going to give away her virtue."

That was true, only he didn't know what kind of woman she truly was, and right now, neither did she. After all, she was singing in a saloon. And she loved her performances there.

"Where is Sadie?"

Tessa led her to the sofa. "Oh, you missed it. Levi proposed to her tonight in front of the entire ballroom, including his mother and Nellie."

A surge of joy swept through Rose. "I'm so happy for her. I just hope that his dreadful mother accepts her."

A laugh escaped from Tessa. "From what Sadie told me, Levi gave his mother no choice if she wanted to remain in their lives."

That made Rose so happy. Betty Griffin could be a very nasty woman and she'd worried about Sadie.

"But the other big spectacle at the ball tonight was your father. When he received word that you had not been found, he asked all the men in his congregation to start searching the town looking for you."

"Oh dear," she said sighing. "I hoped when I unveiled tonight, I would be shunned. And maybe, eventually, I will be."

Tessa shook her head. "What are you talking about?"

"I've been singing at the saloon every night in a disguise

the stage manager and I rigged. Tonight, I unveiled myself, knowing it would ruin my reputation."

"Rose, why would you do that?"

"Because I didn't want to marry that creepy preacher my father found for me. I don't want to be a preacher's wife. And the way he looked at me frightened me."

She watched her friend sink back against the sofa.

"I just hope Sadie will let me stay."

"You know she will," Tessa said. "Seems we're all about to join the Bad Girls' Club."

Just then Miss Tabor walked into the room in her robe, her hair up in a net.

"Rose?"

"Yes, ma'am?"

"What are you doing here? Your father is searching the town for you."

Quickly, she told her the reason she had run away tonight. Frannie stared at her. "Oh dear. Looks like I'm going to have another girl to coach on surviving scandal."

"Yes, I plan on creating scandal. Anything to keep me from being married to a man who frightens me."

Frannie clapped her hands together almost gleefully. The woman seemed to really enjoy scandalous women.

A knock at the door suddenly resounded.

"Quickly, go upstairs," Frannie said. "Let me handle this."

She tossed Tessa a book and the woman opened it like she was reading. When Rose was out of sight, she heard Frannie open the door.

Rose glanced out the window. There were six men on horseback in the yard. She recognized them from her father's congregation. If she had arrived any later, they would have caught her. And now they would probably search the house for her.

"Reverend, what are you doing here at such a late hour? Is something wrong?"

"Sorry, to disturb you, but I thought that maybe my daughter, Rose, might be here. She's having some sort of mental breakdown and her mother and I are worried sick about her."

Mental breakdown? Did he really think he could get away with this? It would explain to society why she was singing in a saloon. It would give him more time to convince the young man to marry her. It would tarnish her as a person who wasn't capable of making a decision. Her parents would have to step in and place her in an appropriate home.

One that included an ugly preacher man.

Her body began to shake violently, her knees knocking, barely holding her up, hands quivering with nervousness. Was she crazy to think she could escape the church?

Frannie turned to Tessa. "Have you seen Rose tonight?"

"No, and I looked all over the ballroom for her. Where is she?"

The man sighed and tried to look in the door. Rose made certain that she was not peeking out through the cracked bedroom door. If he found her, she would be hauled out of here, kicking and screaming by the men she'd seen when she gazed out the window.

Maybe this wasn't going to be such a safe spot after all.

Just then, Sadie and her fiancé walked up to the door. "Reverend Tuttle, why are you here?"

He explained to her that Rose was missing and he thought that maybe she might be here.

With distress, Rose watched as Sadie opened the door and

invited him into the house. "Please come in and let's talk about what is going on. I'm very worried about Rose."

The man frowned and took a step back. "I'm sorry. I can't go in there. You're a young Jezebel, and well, it wouldn't be right for me to be seen in your home with your housemate, in her robe, and your reputation."

Levi turned on the man. "Watch what you say. Sadie is going to be my wife and she is no Jezebel. Do you understand me?"

It was all Rose could do not to giggle out loud.

"Pardon me," the reverend said. "But I can't go in your house."

Oh no, he wouldn't walk in because he considered Sadie's house a den of sin. Could she stay here, after all?

Sadie held out her hands and yelled. "Rose, dear, are you here? Come out if you are. Your father is worried about you."

Rose was not moving. She knew all too well what would happen to her if she left her hiding place. Marriage to a creep was not on her to do list at the moment.

"Sorry, sir, but as you can see, Rose is not here. Please let me know when you find her. I'm most worried about her."

The man grumbled, but then back from the door. "You will tell me if she comes around?"

"Of course."

"My men will be keeping a close watch on the area, searching for her. I don't know why the girl ran off. I found her a nice man to marry. A man of God. She could continue her life of serving the Lord."

It wasn't the serving the Lord that got to Rose. It was serving the men in the congregation and doing their bidding. That was what burned her. And the fact that she wanted to sing. God had given her a wonderful talent and she wanted to share it with the world.

After her father left, she waited another ten minutes, afraid that some stray church member was left staring in the windows trying to catch Sadie in a lie.

Finally, she walked down the stairs. Sadie ran to her. "Thank God you're here. I've been so worried about you. Welcome to the Bad Girls' Club."

CHAPTER 4

*A*fter Levi left, they sat up talking and chatting until the wee hours of the morning, making a plan. This morning when Rose awoke, she went downstairs. It felt odd not to be awakening at home in her own bed.

The ladies were all sitting in the kitchen at the back of the house. Before they had taken their morning coffee and breakfast outdoors on the patio. But not today.

"Good morning," she said as she went for a cup of coffee.

"Don't go near the windows. Your father was serious about men patrolling the area. They are watching the house," Sadie said.

With a sigh, she sank down at the table. What was she going to do? She needed to earn more money to take the train to New York. She knew when she arrived, it would take time to be hired on to the opera.

"I've got to work tonight. How am I going to leave without them seeing me?"

They all stared across the table at each other.

"It's a shame your father didn't build an outbuilding or

something that we could sneak her out through," Tessa said. She glanced at her watch. "Sorry, ladies, I must leave. It's target practice time and then I have to go work in Papa's shop for a while for him. Amazing that I can run his gun shop, but no one thinks a lady should participate in competitive shooting."

"That's because you'd win," Sadie said with a smile.

"You're damn right, I would win. Scared little men who are afraid a woman can outgun them."

"Have a great day, ladies," Tessa said as she walked out the door.

Sadie and Rose remained at the breakfast table, each one deep in thought. "As soon as I earn enough money, I'm leaving for New York."

"You know I'll give you the money you need," Sadie said. "I've heard you sing; you have a great voice."

Her friend was a rich heiress with money left from her father's cattle business. But Rose needed to make it on her own. She didn't want to take her friends' money, because what if she could never pay it back?

"Thank you, but I want to do this on my own. If my father puts too much pressure on me and it appears I'm going to lose, then I'll take you up on your offer."

Shaking her head, Sadie stared at her. "By then, it could be too late. It would be better if we put you on a train today."

In some ways that sounded wonderful, but Rose was unprepared. She had always planned on leaving with her trunks packed. Not sneaking out the window and running for her life. And one of the legitimate ways she earned money was tutoring young girls playing the piano. They were her students that she hated to leave without saying good-bye.

Especially MaryJane. The young girl showed promise, and

she wanted to encourage her and that little bit of money would be just a bit more in her nest egg when she reached New York. But how could she continue to tutor her students when she was considered one of the bad girls in town?

Would they have people waiting at her students' homes to snatch her before she had a chance to bid them farewell?

Why did it have to be this way? She didn't want to leave town, not saying good-bye to the people she cared about. Even her mother, brother, and sister.

"Oh my God," she said. "My sister's baptism is two weeks from Sunday. How can I miss it?"

"Honey, she'll be all right knowing that you're thinking of her."

With a sigh, Rose realized there would be more times like this when she would not be able to participate in family functions. As she would be in New York.

No matter what, she had to be a success. When she returned to Fort Worth, Texas, she wanted to come back as a star. Someone who had escaped and returned a hero.

"I need to go to work tonight. Somehow I have to figure out a way to deceive them all."

Her friend shook her head and started to laugh. "You need a disguise for when you leave the house and one for when you come home. It will have to be two different disguises."

"Or else they will realize it's me," she finished for her friend.

"Yes," Sadie said and then she tilted her head. "Tessa told me that Hayden brought you home from the saloon."

Warmth filled Rose as she thought of the man and how he had kept her safe last night. Sure, his words had been so damn frustrating, but he had redeemed himself when he got them out of the brawl that happened on Main Street.

"I don't know how I feel about him. For the last three months, every night, he's been there, listening to me sing, watching me, staring at me with those blue-as-a-brilliant-sky eyes. And then he kissed me last night."

Sadie grinned. "What did you think?"

"I've never been kissed before, but it felt good."

"Did you get all warm and tingly inside?"

Rose stared at her friend. How had she known? "Yes."

"Sounds to me like you're attracted to him."

Could that be true? She had admired and liked the man from afar until last night.

"But then the first thing he says to me after he realizes who I am is 'Will you be my mistress?'"

Sadie's mouth dropped open. "He didn't. What a bastard."

"I'm not going to be his mistress. Before that statement, I was a little curious, and I loved the way he was different from the rest of the patrons of the saloon. But with one sentence, he managed to destroy every dream I'd had of him."

"Sometimes men don't know how to treat a lady, but surely, I thought he would do better than that."

"Before the night was over, he apologized. Especially when he realized it was never going to happen."

A smile curled on Sadie's face. "You know, he and Levi are good friends."

"Yes, Levi was at the saloon one night with him."

"Tell me how you feel when he glances at you."

Why would Sadie want to know that? She thought back to all the nights he had sat and stared at her while she sang. There was no question that he was different from all the other men. She had never seen him drunk. He didn't hoot and holler at her but sat there gazing like a refined gentleman.

Every night when she left the stage, a strong connection of

excitement filled her, because the last song she stared right back at him, singing it for him.

"Warmth. Like warm honey was poured over my insides. So why did he have to ruin that feeling by trying to make it cheap?"

Sadie reached her hands across the table. "Because he probably thought that because you sang in a saloon, you were just like all the other bar maids. Easy. A bad girl."

That was probably true. Any cowboy in the bar would probably think she could very easily be had, but they were all wrong. She may be considered a bad girl because she sang in the bar, but that didn't mean she would just give herself to any man like a common whore.

"When he learned I was the preacher's daughter, he suddenly decided he would make me a bad girl?"

Her friend started to laugh. "Probably. Men want to tarnish a woman's good name. They like turning us into bad girls."

"Well, this bad girl is not going down because of a man. She's going down because of desire not to marry some preacher man who will never let her fulfill her dream. Who would probably abuse her if given the chance."

Rose got up to pour herself another cup of coffee.

"Maybe Hayden is your ticket to New York. He owns a railroad. I bet he could help you get there," Sadie said.

"No, like I said earlier, I'm doing this on my own. I would never use your money or his railroad unless I had no choice. And even then, I would pay you back."

"Honey, I don't think your father is going to give you an option. They're going to try to make you look unstable, like you're mad. It's a mark against him as a preacher to have his daughter run away. When you're ready, let me know. I'll have the funds ready for you to leave town."

A trickle of unease spiraled through Rose. "They may even be watching the railroad station."

"True. It's not going to take him long to find you."

"Let me think about it, Sadie."

The image of Hayden came to mind. Why was she thinking of him now when she should be planning her escape out of town?

CHAPTER 5

$\mathcal{H}$ ayden strolled through the grand lobby of the Griffin Hotel, Levi's business. He ran up the stairs to his friend's office on the third floor. At the landing, he paused to glance down to see the people milling about the fancy interior before being escorted to their rooms.

He had made a mess of things and he knew it. Whatever possessed him to ask Rose to be his mistress, he had no idea.

But for months now, he'd watched her, dreamed of her, lusted after her and wanted her with a fierceness he couldn't seem to deny. And when he realized who she was, he knew that she was ruined. It seemed like the logical solution, but he'd been wrong to mention it.

And the lady let him know rather quickly that wasn't an option.

What woman wanted to be kissed and then the first words out of a man's mouth to be when can I fuck you? He'd made a serious mistake and he hoped she would give him the chance to make up for his stupidity.

Hopefully, he had made amends by rescuing her last night.

But she threatened to tell her brother what he'd said. And if someone said something like that to one of his sisters, they would be meeting him in the streets.

So what made it all right for him to ask her an inappropriate question?

Because he had to have her. And that was the only way possible he could see them being together. His father was pressuring him to find some rich society woman and marry her. But he could not think of anyone he could promise eternity to. All he could think of was Rose.

And his father would never accept Mr. Tuttle's daughter, a saloon singer, in their family. She didn't have money. She didn't have society behind her. She would bring nothing with her, not even a small dowry, and he would consider her after their fortune.

For some reason, Hayden didn't see it that way.

Suddenly, he realized Levi's secretary was standing in front of him.

"Yes," the man said, staring at him like he was worried.

"Is Levi available?"

"Who is asking?"

"Hayden Lee. Tell him it's urgent."

"Just a moment," the man said, his eyes widening at the recognition of his name.

When your family owned the largest railroad in Texas, people paid attention. And yet sometimes coming from a well-to-do family was a burden. Why couldn't he marry who he wanted? Why did he have to worry about how his actions could affect the reputation of the people he loved?

Why couldn't people leave him alone and let him live his life?

"Hayden, come in," Levi said, stepping to the door. "We

missed you at the ball last night. Did you hear that Sadie and I are engaged to be married?"

"No, I'm sorry, I missed your announcement. Congratulations! I'm happy that Sadie said yes. How is your mother handling the fact that you're going to marry her nemesis?"

Levi motioned for him to take a seat as he moved around behind his desk.

The man's office was elegant and refined for a businessman, and Hayden was happy that Levi's hotels seemed to be prospering.

The man laughed. "My mother will always be a challenge. But you know I decided that Sadie is who I want in my life and I gave my sweet mother an ultimatum. Stay out of our lives. Mention us in your column and you're dead to us."

In Hayden's life, that would never work. It wasn't his mother, but his father, who was pushing him to find the perfect socialite whose family also was well-to-do and that together the families could combine their business resources.

This was what he hated.

Levi frowned and gazed at him. "You don't look so happy. What's wrong?"

"I wish I had your courage. You know what kind of man my father is."

"Yes, he should have married my mother," Levi said. "What happened?"

"You know he wants me to find a rich socialite and marry."

Shaking his head, Levi gave a little chuckle. "And you're still crazy about Mystery Flower."

"Yes, but now I know that Mystery Flower is really Rose Tuttle."

Unable to sit a moment longer, Hayden jumped up from the chair and began to pace the office. Going to a credenza, he let his fingers slide across the smooth wood. "You should have seen her last night. As she sang the last song, she slowly unwrapped the scarf that hid her face from us. And when she removed it, her hair spilled down her back. All those glorious brunette curls falling down to her waist."

With a groan, he knew at that moment he had to have her. He stopped for a moment and glanced at Levi shaking his head. "And then I totally fucked it up."

"What did you do?"

"I went backstage to ask her to escort her home and she agreed. But then I asked her to be my mistress."

A groan came from Levi and he face palmed his forehead.

"Why in the world would you ask an innocent, the preacher's daughter, to be your mistress?"

"Because I knew she could never be my wife and I have to have her."

"Well, you're not going to get her like that. Don't you realize why she took off her disguise? She's trying to save herself from a loveless marriage and instead you offered her something even worse. She must hate men."

It was true. He'd been so stupid. When Rose told him why she was running away, he'd known he really had chosen the wrong moment to ask her to be his mistress. One man was trying to marry her off and the other just wanted to take her home and brand her as his. Not good.

"What do I do now? I apologized and she asked me how I would feel if someone said that to my sisters?"

Shaking his head, Levi laughed. "After you dropped her off, you missed her father and the men from his congregation coming to Sadie's house looking for her."

Hayden felt his heart skip a beat. If she returned to her father's, he would never see her again. Because her father

28

would lock her up until the day she said *I do* to the man she despised.

"Did he find her?"

"No, but he promised to continue looking for her."

"How will she get to the saloon tonight? How will she sing if her father's men grab her, and you know they will the first chance they get. We'll never see her again."

Levi smiled. "That's where you come in, dear friend. This is where you can make yourself indebted to her. Tonight after she sings, tell her that she will never be safe at Sadie's. And that's not a lie, she never will be. But if she stayed with you, then no one would suspect."

For a moment, Hayden felt excitement stirring through him and he smiled at his friend and then he shook his head. "She would never agree to come stay with me. She'll think I'm just going to ruin her."

Tapping his fingers on the desk, Levi grinned. "No, you must be a complete gentleman. You have to prove to her that you would never cross boundaries and try to seduce her. She needs a safe place and that you are there to help her. You have to become her hero. Her rescuer. And then…"

A smile spread across his face and he smiled at his friend. "What if her father and his men are waiting outside the saloon?"

"She needs a disguise going in and out of the White Elephant. Or a diversion. But I don't know if her father has learned that she's singing at the saloon yet. What man is going to tell his faith leader that he's been going to a saloon and happened to see his daughter there?"

With relief, Hayden sunk down into the chair. This was why he admired his friend. The man had a keen mind. "Are you going to Sadie's this evening?"

"Yes," Levi said. "We're going to discuss wedding plans."

"Tell Rose that I will pick her up at seven to take her to the saloon. Tell her to have her bags packed."

"No, you need to discuss with her the idea of staying at your place. And, Hayden, she has no bags. She has nothing but the clothes on her back. The woman crawled out of a window and ran to the saloon."

Hayden grinned. "I can help with that."

CHAPTER 6

*R*ose was upstairs when she heard a knock on the
door. Dressed like a man, she wore britches that
Sadie had borrowed, a hat, and they had taken a charcoal
pencil and drawn a mustache on her face. And yet the sound
of the knock terrified her.

For a second, she was transported back in time. The
memory of her father slapping her mother, telling her she was
a bad influence on the congregation and that if she didn't
become a better wife, he would find another.

Her mother had left the room crying.

Later that day while she dressed to attend the Cattleman's
Ball, unbeknownst to her, Pastor John Moore and her father
were downstairs working out the details of their marriage.

When her father called her, she'd walked into the room
and stood before the two men. It was then she noticed how
Pastor Moore gazed at her like she was candy. They told her
of the engagement and how they would announce their
pending marriage tonight at the Cattleman's Ball.

When her father was called from the room, they were left alone. Pastor Moore stood and began to walk around her in a circle, speaking to her softly.

"You will always obey me and follow the Lord's commandments or I will put the rod to you and you'll think twice about sitting. You will be my wife, my helpmate, and I will demand complete surrender to me."

He grabbed her buttocks and squeezed. "I'm going to enjoy making certain you understand that I'm your husband, your master."

The sound of the door closing, brought Rose back to the present and a shiver rippled through her. She would die rather than marry that man

What if they were waiting for her just outside the house? What if they recognized her and forcibly removed her from the carriage? But she couldn't just sit here in this room. She had to take a chance if she wanted to live her dream.

She listened to the voices downstairs. It was Levi.

"Rose, come down," Sadie called. "Levi has worked out a plan to get you to the saloon."

Then she heard heated whispering and knew that Sadie was not all right with what was going on. What had Levi planned?

When she came down the stairs, Levi looked up at her and grinned. "Now that's a disguise."

"I don't like this idea at all," Sadie said as she turned to Rose. "Hayden Lee is coming to pick you up."

A smile crossed her face. "It's all right. In fact, it might be a good idea."

The man knew better than to cross her and she still carried her trusty knife in her pocket. It was her protection from boisterous cowboys wanting to reach her on stage and also it protected her as she snuck back home each night.

No man had tested her yet, but she was willing to bet that sooner or later, someone would.

But now she had a much farther walk to reach Sadie's house at night. It could be dangerous trying to come back here. Maybe she could get a hotel room, but the owners knew her father and it was almost a guarantee they would tell him her location.

No one wanted to cross Reverend Tuttle because he would tell the congregation to boycott their business.

She would just have to do her best to walk in the darkness back to Sadie's.

Just then, she heard Hayden's carriage pull up to the house.

"It's going to be all right," Levi told her. "Hayden will protect you."

"But who is going to protect me from him?" she asked.

Levi smiled and she knew she was right.

"If he so much as touches you, you tell him he will have me to answer to," Sadie said. She tugged the hat down over Rose's face even farther. "Please be careful. I don't want to learn that your father found you."

Knowing that this was what she must do if she wanted to continue to sing each night, she hugged her friend. "I will."

Turning, she opened the door and glanced out. Not seeing anyone, she tried to move like an older man to the carriage. The driver held the door open for her and she climbed in and looked out the window. So far so good.

"Good evening," Hayden said, glancing at her from the other side of the carriage. "Your disguise is good, though I never thought about how you would look in pants."

She stared at him, not knowing what to say and chose to ignore his comments. It had been difficult putting on men's clothing, but she had no choice. "Good evening."

"My brother said to tell you he's going to injure your ass," she said.

He laughed. "You haven't spoken to your brother or you would not be returning to the saloon tonight. I, for one, am glad that you're going to continue singing."

"Until I leave for New York," she said.

In the darkened carriage, she watched his eyes widen at the news.

"New York? Whatever for?"

"I want to sing in the opera," she said, joy bubbling up and filling her at the very thought of appearing on a stage with an audience of normal people, not drunken cowboys at her feet.

"You'd be excellent," he said. "That's a big dream for a small woman like yourself. How are you going to get there?"

She wondered if he was making fun of her, but for some reason, she didn't think so. Women had dreams just like men. Some were of a home and family and others were outrageous like her own.

"By train. How else?" she said.

"You do realize my family owns one of the largest rail-roads in Texas," he told her.

"Yes, but I'm not traveling in Texas. I want to go to New York."

They were driving through the streets of Fort Worth. At this early hour, things seemed calm. A tinny piano played in the distance as they neared Hell's Half Acre where the saloons were. Cowboys strolled down Main Street, their hats pulled low, guns strapped on their hips. Ready for action.

"When you get ready to leave for New York, let me know. I can arrange for you to have a comfortable car," he said.

A car? A whole railroad car? Did he think she was made of money? That would probably cost more than all the money she had saved to travel.

Knowing she would never ask him, she nodded. "Thank you."

As they pulled up to the back entrance of the White Elephant Saloon, Hayden peered out the window before his driver hopped down from the bucket area of the elegant carriage.

He opened the door. "No one in sight, sir."

"Thanks, George. Come back around midnight and pick us up."

"I can walk home," she said to him.

"Like hell," he replied. "You'll be picked up by one of your father's men as soon as you walk out of the Acre."

She frowned at him as he helped her alight from the carriage. Standing in the alley, he smiled at her and then gave her a quick kiss on the lips. Warmth flowed like a river through her and she was stunned. Why did she enjoy this man? Because he believed in her?

"Sing for me tonight. Have a great show and I'll see you inside."

She gazed at him feeling uncomfortable and yet she melted at his words. *Sing for me tonight.* Didn't she sing for him every night? It felt that way sometimes.

Turning on her heel, she entered the back entrance to the saloon. Time to put the outside world away and concentrate on performing her best for the rowdy cowboys who wouldn't know one word of the opera songs she sometimes sang.

But all the ballads they knew by heart. As she entered the

dressing area, a tingle zinged down her spine and she gasped as fear seized her.

Her mother sat in the dressing area gazing at her like she couldn't believe what she was seeing.

"Hello, Rose. Is this what a young Christian woman should be doing?"

CHAPTER 7

*R*ose felt the blood drain from her body, her knees began to knock. She loved her mother. She loved her and had watched her be treated terribly by some of the members of her father's congregation. Her own father often times abused his wife. And yet she wanted her daughter to become a preacher's wife.

"Mother, what are you doing here? Is Papa with you?"

Wearing the plain gray dress she always wore, her mother's face appeared tired. It was like she had grown older overnight. Could her mother have worried about her?

"No, your father has not learned his daughter is singing in a saloon, yet. Instead, one of the older gentlemen came to me and told me where you could be found. He was trying to protect you."

It was not like her mother to keep secrets from her father and she knew that probably tonight she was giving her one last chance to change her wicked ways. One last chance before they railed hell and damnation against her.

"Mother, I can't marry that man. Did you see the way he

was staring at me, like he was looking at me with my clothes off? Like he wanted to hurt me."

With a roll of her eyes, her mother pursed her lips and then she almost growled at her.

"And you think the men in this establishment are not doing the same? All men look at women that way. At least he is a man of God. And sometimes men inflict pain on their wives."

No. Why would a man who loved you hurt you? You didn't hurt the people you loved.

Was she wrong? Sure, the men in the saloon stared at her. Some even tried to convince her to meet them afterward, but she let them all know right up front that she was not interested. Her only purpose was to sing in the saloon. Nothing else.

Her mother's tone softened. "You're our daughter. You are a child of God. You need to stop this and come home right now," her mother commanded. "Before you lose the man your father has chosen for you."

Doubts assailed her like a storm bombarding her. Maybe she would never sing opera. Maybe she would never become a famous person on the stage. Maybe she was meant to just sing in the church choir.

Maybe she was just a young girl chasing a foolish dream.

"But I don't want to be a preacher's wife. Mother, I've seen the way some people in the congregation treat you. I've witnessed the backstabbing, the gossip. I've seen how Papa puts the church before you. That's not what I want."

Her mother stood and took hold of her hands. She squeezed them hard. "What you've seen goes on in every church. Women are to obey their husbands. We are to be meek, seen and not heard. Their comments don't bother me. I am shielded by the love of God."

Rose had grown up in the church, she believed, but she felt this calling for a different life. Was she wrong to feel that way?

"Now grab your things. We're going home," her mother said, not giving her another chance to argue.

Like a dutiful daughter, Rose picked up her reticule and walked out of the dressing room door following her mother obediently.

When they stepped into the hallway, she heard the chants.

"Rose, Rose, Rose, Rose," the men hollered.

Stunned, she stopped and listened to them. That was her audience. That was her crowd and they were expecting her to perform for them tonight. They wanted to hear her sing.

Her body filled with unexpected joy. Her legs refused to move.

"Rose," her mother said sternly.

This was her calling. Her life. And God had given her this voice to share with the people. Maybe she never would sing opera, but she would not know until she tried. And she had to go to New York and audition.

"I can't. I'm sorry, Momma. I know you don't understand. But I'm being called to sing. I can feel it in my bones. This is what I'm supposed to do with my life. You'll go back and tell Papa where I'm at. I know you will, but I can't marry that man. It would be wrong. I'm supposed to sing."

Grabbing her mother, she hugged her. "I'm going to New York. You can try to stop me, but I will run, sooner or later. I'm going to succeed. Even if I never become a big star, I'm going to sing on stage."

Turning, she fled back into the dressing room and began to remove her male disguise. Grabbing the dress she performed in, she hurried, eager to sing for her audience. But this time, the mask, the veil, was gone. For the first time ever, she would go out on stage and perform as Rose Tuttle.

That was her audience calling to her. And Hayden would be waiting for her to sing to him. This was her dream.

CHAPTER 8

*H*ayden sat once again in the saloon, mesmerized by Rose's talent. Her voice was like a fine whiskey, smooth and silky and warm going down. One that left you craving more.

For some reason, she had been late coming out on stage and he'd almost gone to the back to check on her, but when she came out, she performed more relaxed and gave the best performance he'd ever seen.

She was a star in the making. One that he believed would do well in New York. And he had the means to take her there.

But how was she going to accept him telling her she should stay with him. She was going to think he was only trying to get her to sleep with him and he wasn't. Though if that was the final result, he'd be more than happy to oblige.

Just thinking of the two of them in his big bed, naked, was enough to make him hard. Yes, he wanted Rose, but he wanted what he couldn't have. Something that his family would never approve of. And yet, he knew she would not relent and be his mistress either.

Of that, he was certain.

After her performance, he waited for her outside her dressing room door. She came out smiling. The saloon owner handed her a wad of bills.

"Rose, tonight we made more money in one night than ever before. Thank you," Randal said smiling. "And please don't leave us anytime soon."

Reedy music came from the piano player still playing for the remaining cowboys who would drink until they closed up for the night. Hayden felt an urgency to get her out of here before trouble exploded.

She grinned. "After tonight, I suggest you have extra security. Some fool let my mother in, and after our conversation, I'm sure she ran home to tell my papa where I am."

"Damn, if I find out who, they're fired," Randal said, shaking his head. "Truly, I hoped we could avoid your father's wrath."

"Afraid not," Rose said. "I'll sing for as long as I can, but eventually, I'm leaving for New York."

The man smiled. "Understand. When I see you, we'll know you're still here."

"Yes," she said and gave him a quick hug. "Thank you for giving me the confidence to sing onstage. That means a lot."

"You're going to be a star someday," he told her. "Just remember you sang here first."

"I will."

Hayden felt his chest tighten, the need to get her out of here even more urgent. Even now the men were probably gathering to ambush them.

"We better go, Rose," he said, gripping her elbow. "We need to get you home before they come looking for you."

"You're right," she said.

When they reached the door, he peeked outside and saw his carriage waiting for them. He hustled her out, not bothering to wait for George to open the carriage door. With a shove, he pushed her inside and then followed.

When he felt the carriage moving, he glanced out the window behind them. No one was following them.

He turned and faced her. "Tonight's performance was exceptional. You sang even better than normal."

She smiled. "I felt free tonight. My mother was waiting for me in the dressing room. I almost left with her, but then I heard the men chanting my name. It was surreal. And in that moment, I knew I would regret for the rest of my life leaving with her."

Who in the hell had let her mother in? If he had to buy that damn saloon and start managing it, he would. She would be safe at all costs.

"Maybe we shouldn't go back to Sadie's. I'm afraid they're going to realize that you're staying with her and they will be waiting for you there."

Chewing her bottom lip, he could see that she was carefully considering his words. "Where would I go? To a hotel? I'm sure they would contact my father in the middle of the night and he would drag me out of there. At least at Sadie's if I can get inside, I feel safe."

"What if you stayed with me."

Laughter filled the carriage and he knew exactly what she was thinking.

"I have a big home with four guest bedrooms. You could have whichever one you choose. My servants are there to cook and take care of you during the day. Every night, I would make certain you made it to the saloon safely. It makes perfect sense. And who would know you were there?"

In the flickering shadows, he gazed at her.

"No one would ever think you were bold enough to stay with me."

"Who is going to protect me from you?" she asked, raising her pointed chin at him in defiance.

Oh, it was true, he wanted her so badly, he could hardly stand it, but he would. No one would ever accuse him of not being a gentleman.

Bowing his head for a moment, he wanted to curse himself for that stupid comment he made the other night. With determination, he raised his head and stared into her beautiful dark brown eyes.

"I'm not going to lie to you. There is something about you that has enthralled me. I want you. But you have said no and I'm not a man who takes a woman against her will. Nothing will happen until you say yes. If you never say yes, then at least you'll be safe."

She bit her bottom lip again, contemplating his words.

"I'm a man of my word. So far I've kissed you once passionately and once chastely, though you're bewitching and I would love to explore that lip that you insist on chewing."

A streetlamp flickered along the road and he watched as she held her hands in her lap tightly. The light reflected the tenseness on her face.

"My reputation would be completely ruined if anyone learned I was staying with you. I think it's best that I stay with Sadie."

"You're not safe with her," he said. "I can offer you protection. Yes, you're right, your reputation would be ruined, but then again, your character is in shambles even now. When people learn you're singing at the saloon, no one is going to believe that you're an innocent."

She raised her head and held it high. "Then they would be wrong."

If what she said was true, that meant she was a virgin. And that made things even more difficult. With her living under his roof, he would have a very hard time keeping his hands off her. But he would not defile a virgin for his own pleasure.

They turned the corner to Sadie's house and stared in stunned silence at the men on horses sitting outside her house with torches.

"Dear God," she whispered staring at the sight.

Hayden opened the window. "Don't stop," he told the driver. "Keep going."

While the horsemen appeared to be keeping a respectable distance from the house, there was no way his carriage could get in there and drop her off safely. She would have to walk through them to reach the house.

"Rose, you can't even reach the door. You'll be safer with me."

Shaking her head, she stared at him. "Will I?"

"Yes," he said and prayed that he could keep his promise.

CHAPTER 9

$\mathcal{R}$ose was amazed at the large, brick, two-story home with lamps glowing in the windows. The carriage rolled through an open gate, pulled to the back of the house under an awning and came to a stop. The driver opened the door and Hayden stepped out and helped Rose alight.

Just glancing around at the perfectly groomed gardens, she knew she'd never been to such a fine home.

With a stunning awareness, she realized she had nothing with her. Sadie had loaned her a nightgown, but she had no other clothing. No clean clothes, no sleeping gown, only the men's clothing on her back.

Standing there, she glanced around and felt the urge to run. As if he sensed her hesitancy, he took her hand and led her up the steps into the house.

"I'm sorry, you're not going through the front entrance, but it's better this way. No one can see you."

Licking her lips, she followed him into a small mud room.

He led her through the kitchen, a dining room, and then into a main room that had a fireplace and couches and chairs for guest. An opulent room that was stately.

The man lived like a king.

"Let me sit for a moment," she said, nerves suddenly overcoming her. Maybe she should just tell him she couldn't do this and walk out the door. But where would she go?

"Would you like something to drink? A glass of sherry or tea or water?"

"No, I just need a moment," she said as she sank on one of the plush couches. The man must have more money than Satan. She'd never been in such an elegant home. Even the richest member of the church didn't live in something this nice.

A thick rug covered the wooden floors and an ornate table was in front of her with a vase of flowers and a newspaper.

"Melody is the head housekeeper. If you need anything, she can help you. Or Sandra is also available for you. I know you are without clothes, so I thought that tomorrow we would go shopping. Or if you're afraid to be seen, I could have a dressmaker come to the house."

She shook her head. "No. I'm not a charity case for you to take on."

A chuckle escaped from him and he walked over to the liquor cabinet and poured himself some kind of liquor. What if he became drunk?

Sitting in his home, she felt vulnerable. Sure she had seen him for months, but two days ago was the first time they'd spoken. She hardly knew him and what would she do if he tried something?

It was late. After midnight and she was starting to feel

panic. Why had she agreed to this? Surely, there must have been some way for her to get inside Sadie's home.

He sank onto a sofa across from her. As he sipped his drink, he smiled.

"Rose, I have more than enough money and I would love to dress you. I'm not asking anything in return. Let me purchase for you the things you need."

There was so much that she needed. And being a preacher's daughter, they seldom had everything. And new clothes... she had never experienced, wearing only hand-me-downs. Even the gowns she wore to the balls were second hand.

"I'll think about it," she said, not liking the idea of owing him anything. "Tomorrow is piano practice for my favorite student."

As much as she knew it would endanger her, she wanted to see MaryJane one more time. The girl was going to be a great pianist and she just wanted to give her encouragement.

"Will her parents let her meet you somewhere?"

With a sigh, Rose shook her head. "Her parents are the strictest in our congregation. Once they hear that I'm singing in a saloon, they will never let me see her again. Not to mention the money they pay me for teaching her."

They paid her twice what her other parents paid. That well-earning job was suddenly stripped away. Somehow she would write MaryJane a note, knowing she would never be allowed to see her again.

And she feared if she wasn't careful, she would not be able to get inside the saloon.

He pulled out his pocket watch. "It's late. We both need to rest. I'm sure tomorrow will bring us some kind of drama. It's time we went to bed."

Fear struck inside her chest. "No, I told you I would not sleep with you or have sex."

A smiled crossed his tired face, his sapphire eyes twinkled in the dim light. His dimples appeared and she realized she'd never considered how truly handsome he was until now. "I'm going to sleep in my room at the end of the hall. You're going to choose which room you wish to sleep in."

He rose from the couch and walked over to her.

"I think I'll stay down here," she replied.

A chuckle escaped him. "No, you need your rest. Come on. At the top of the stairs, we'll be parting ways."

She swallowed and took his offered hand. Her knees were shaking as she climbed the stairs with him, terrified of what would happen next.

When they reached the top of the stairs, he kissed her on the forehead. "Rose, you have no idea how glad I am that you are staying with me in my home. You make me very happy."

The feel of his lips on her forehead had her heart skittering inside her chest.

"Just ring the bell if you need anything," he said. "Each bedroom has one."

"Thank you," she said as she watched him walk down the hallway to a room at the end.

She waited until he went inside his bedroom before she glanced in each of the bedrooms. When she opened the room third bedroom the farthest from his, she walked in and shut the door. The blue colors of the wall and the flowered bed coverlet drew her attention. It was a cheery room that made her smile.

Here, she would do her best to sleep. Pushing a chair up against the door, she blocked the entrance before she pulled back the covers, removed her shoes, and crawled into bed fully clothed.

As she lay in the quiet house, she couldn't help but think of the choices she'd made today. Though she loved her family, the choice to continue singing made her happy. Somehow she was determined to get to New York. To fulfill her dream.

Someday soon, she planned on leaving Fort Worth behind.

CHAPTER 10

*H*ayden got very little sleep knowing that she was only doors away from him, and yet he hoped she rested comfortably.

Sitting at breakfast the next morning, he had told his housekeeper that she was sleeping in one of the guest rooms upstairs and that she was to be given anything she asked for. The woman gazed at him like she understood, but her face was void of emotion. Like she was doing her best not to pass judgement. While his staff was very trustworthy, he hoped they would not tell anyone of her whereabouts.

If he didn't have an important meeting with the board this morning, he would not have gone into the office, but he was in charge of the finances, and at board meetings, his presence was required. And his father would become suspicious if he didn't show up.

Suddenly the front door to his home opened and his mother walked through the door.

"Good morning, son, I knew you would be up and so I just dropped in to check on you."

Like a whirlwind, his mother spun into the room in a beautiful yellow dress, a basket of cookies in her hand.

"I brought you your favorite cookies."

Shit! Shit! Shit! What if Rose came downstairs? He had told his staff that no one was to know she was here. And while he trusted his mother to keep his secrets, he didn't know how she would react to a single, young woman living in his house.

A woman he would like nothing better than for her to find her way to his bed. One taste. That's all he wanted and then he could put her out of his mind.

"Good morning, Mother," he said, rising and kissing her on the cheek. "What brings you by this morning? Sit and have some coffee."

His mother sank down in a chair across from him. She placed the basket of cookies on the table.

"Well, I know you have that important meeting this morning so I wanted to see if you would like to come have dinner with us tonight."

He thought for a moment, and then shook his head. "Not possible."

Rose would need to be at the saloon early, before the crowds began to arrive. Before someone caught her going in the back door. No matter what time they arrived, it was going to be difficult.

She frowned. "We've not seen you in ages. You're always so busy out and about. I would think we would see more about you in the society pages. But again, it is that dreadful Betty Griffin who writes that column. About the only way you would get in the paper was if you were doing something dreadful."

At any moment, he could be exposed. It wasn't so much his reputation that he worried about, but Rose's.

"Let's hope that's a column I never appear in," he said, wondering if he should talk to Levi, but not wanting to put him on the spot. His friend had enough problems with his scandalmonger mother.

"How are my sisters?"

"Sara thinks she's in love. But then again, she's in love with someone new every other week. Gloria is concentrating on her studies. I swear that girl will be the first female president, if they allowed such a thing. Joan and Judith are enjoying the summer. Beth, God love her, is taking piano lessons, and Cissie has decided she would rather be a man."

He started chuckling. His sisters ranged in age from twenty to eight and the youngest, Cissie was pure minx. Joan and Judith were twins who created more mischief than his family could sometimes handle. Someday one of them would end up in the gossip column and he'd be tempted to kill whoever put them there.

"They miss seeing you," she said, rubbing his arm. "But then so do I."

"Sorry, Mother, I've been really busy," he said, thinking of the nights he had sat at the saloon listening to Rose.

As the oldest, he'd been the first to make his fortune and move out of the house. Sara would probably be next, though he couldn't imagine her being married. Women were odd creatures and he loved each and every one of his sisters. And would protect them with his life.

His comment to Rose came back to his mind and he wanted to groan.

"Mother, I made a mess of something."

She made a motion for his maid to bring her a cup of coffee.

"I knew something was going on. A mother just knows these things. What happened?"

Was he wrong to tell her about Rose? Yet if anyone would defend and protect him, it was his mother. It was better that she knew what was going on before she learned from someone else. Because any day now, this situation could explode.

And then everyone would be talking about him and Rose.

"For months now, I've been going to this saloon and listening to this singer. Mother, she has the voice of an angel. She's no ordinary singer, but rather someone I could see being on the national stage. Maybe in New York. Maybe at the opera."

He paused and glanced down and then looked up into his mother's eyes. "I really care about her a lot. I'm infatuated with her. At first, I didn't know who she was. She wore a disguise, because she didn't anyone to know her name. But two nights ago, she removed her mask. It was Rose Tuttle."

His mother jerked back. "Reverend Tuttle's daughter?"

"Yes," he said with a sigh. "Mother, I can't stop thinking about her. She's beautiful and I could listen to her sing all day long."

His mother's eyes widened.

"This is really unusual for you," she said. "But what did you do wrong?"

He sighed, knowing his mother would not understand, but he was going to tell her anyway.

"I asked her to become my mistress," he said.

"Hayden Thorton Lee, you were raised better than that," she said, her tone filled with disappointment.

How could he explain to his mother that he only wanted to get Rose into his bed? One taste and yet now she was living under his roof and the temptation was almost more than he could bear. Not something you said to your mother.

"You're right, I was, and no, Rose did not take too kindly to it. In fact, she turned and walked away from me."

His mother grinned. "I like her already. But I heard she was missing."

He swallowed. "Her father has found her a man to marry and she ran away not wanting to become a preacher's wife."

Picking up her coffee, she sipped from the hot cup. "Well, I can certainly understand why she feels that way. Most preachers' wives are the nicest women and they're treated badly. Of course, she doesn't want to marry a preacher."

Would his mother understand when he told her that she was living under his roof?

"Last night, when I took her home to her friend Sadie King's home, there were men on horses surrounding the home waiting for Rose to appear. They were not going to let her into Sadie's house. She had nowhere else to go."

She gave a little snort and shook her head. "So you, my fine son, brought her here to your home."

How did the woman know?

"Yes, I did," he said.

"Did you sleep with her?"

Stunned at his mother's crudeness, he laughed.

"No, but not because I didn't want to. She refused me. In fact, that was a condition for her staying here."

His mother leaned back in her chair and stared at him. "This is the first and only woman, that I know of, that you've been so keen on. More interested in than any other time in your life. While I would not have chosen a singer for you, she seems to have grabbed your heart."

It was true.

"Where is she? Why are you hiding her from me?"

"She's asleep in one of the guest rooms," he said. "She needs clothes. She has nothing but the men's disguise she wore to the saloon last night. My plans were to take her shopping, but she refused to let me pay for anything. How can I help her when she keeps refusing me?"

His mother grinned. "Oh, I'm so glad I came here today. This is just the sort of thing I love."

What? Watching her son be miserable because the woman he adored was sleeping under his roof or because he needed her to take her shopping?

"So you'll take her shopping?"

"Oh, how I do love spending a man's money. Of course, I will. And it will give us a chance to get acquainted. Somehow I get the feeling this woman is going to be important in your life."

Like sunshine, joy filled him. "Mother, I knew you would feel that way, but Papa has been after me to marry an heiress."

She reached across the table and took his hand. "Your father would marry his bank account if he could. Leave him to me. If this is the girl you have decided on, then you know I will love and accept her. Your sisters will love and accept her. Your father—he's a hard sell. And he hates Reverend Tuttle."

Hayden smiled. "Thank you, Mother. Now I must get to my meeting. Do your best to stay hidden. We don't need her father learning that she's here at my house."

"Oh, I'll do my best, son. I want to get to know this girl. She could be my newest daughter."

Could he marry Rose? All along, he thought his family would never accept her, but his mother was ready to open her arms wide. His father would probably have nothing to do with her.

His father would never approve of her or him moving to New York.

CHAPTER 11

*A*fter being stressed for two days and staying up late at Sadie's, Rose slept like a lamb. With a chair braced against the door, she had fallen into a deep sleep until sun rays filled her room.

It was late.

Now, in men's clothing, she rose from the bed. After a quick spit bath, she hurried down the stairs. The house was silent. Where was Hayden?

Walking into the dining room, she saw a beautiful woman sat at the table, reading a newspaper. She glanced up at Rose and smiled.

"Good morning. You must be Rose," she said, standing and holding out her hand. "I'm Hayden's mother, Virginia Lee."

Fear gripped Rose. His mother would think the worst of her as she gripped her outstretched hand.

"Rose Tuttle. Nice to meet you," she whispered, staring.

"Please sit, and Melody will bring you your breakfast. I stopped by this morning and Hayden told me all about your situation."

A tremor of unease filled Rose. This was Hayden's mother. The woman must think the absolute worst about her.

After sinking into a chair, she took the cup of coffee the maid brought her. "Would you like eggs?"

"Yes, please," she said, realizing she was starving. She had not eaten supper last night, and this morning, her stomach growled.

For a moment, the older woman sat there contemplating her. "My son tells me you're a singer."

The woman knew she sang in a saloon. Women in saloons were considered taboo. Fallen women who did despicable things with men. Not women in the church.

"Yes, I grew up singing in the church choir. But I wanted more. The saloon owner hired me for one night. After that first time, I've sang almost every night for the last three months. At first, I wore a disguise, so no one would know who I was, but now that's over."

"How did you get there every night?"

"I snuck out of the house and took the back streets to reach the saloon."

"How dangerous to sneak out every night and no one knew?"

"No, ma'am," she said, thinking of the knife she carried in her pants pocket for protection.

His mother smiled at her and nodded. "As women, we're sometimes put in a precarious position. What are your plans?"

How interesting that his mother wanted to know.

"As soon as I earn enough money, I want to go to New York. There, I want to audition for the opera."

Her dreams were laid out in the open and she gazed at the older lady, not ashamed of what she hoped to accomplish.

His mother sat back. "Wow. That's very ambitious."

The maid set a plate of eggs in front of her and while Rose tried not to devour them, she was starving.

How could his mother like her? She was a runaway and she sang in a saloon. Plus, she was sleeping in her son's house, unchaperoned. She must think her a complete slut. A bad girl of the very worst kind.

"I must tell you that I am not a saloon girl nor will I be one for your son."

The woman threw back her head, her brunette curls shaking as she laughed. "You must be an innocent who has not been around men long. My son is completely infatuated with you. I've never seen him act this way about a woman before. He did say you refused to sleep with him."

"Yes."

Happiness coursed through her and yet she couldn't get involved with a man. Not even Hayden if she wished to fulfill her dreams.

"My biggest concern is that you're going to break his heart. Especially if your plans are to go to New York. I fear you'll leave him dejected and bereft."

How could she respond when her dreams were to sing in the opera? It wasn't that she didn't care for Hayden, she did. But there was no way she could continue to live here in Fort Worth with her father seeking her.

"I care about Hayden. He's been so sweet to me and rescued me twice. If I were going to stay here, he would be who I would choose. But I doubt that a man like Hayden would ever pick a poor preacher's daughter. He needs a rich debutante or society woman. My reputation has been ruined. He needs a woman with a spotless name."

His mother sighed. "That's what his father wants and expects. But sometimes as parents, we don't always get what we want." She shrugged. "Reputations are often ruined by rumor and innuendo. Don't worry about what his father is planning. I hear your father has found a preacher for you to marry."

Rose shuddered. "Have you ever looked at someone and just knew they were not a good person?"

Mrs. Lee nodded. "Yes. Always trust your instincts."

"My instincts said run. The man is vile, despicable, and I had to get away. Even if I didn't want to go to New York, I would never marry that man."

Just thinking of him made her shudder. The way his eyes seemed to have no soul and yet lust radiated from them. How could her mother agree to her marrying such a man?

"You're safe for now," Mrs. Lee said, gazing at her with concern. "And we have a shopping trip planned."

"I told Hayden I would not accept his money."

The woman smiled. "Honey, when you've been around as long as I have and a man gives you free rein with his purse, you take it. We're going shopping and when we're finished, you'll have a fabulous wardrobe to wear in New York."

How could she accept this? It was too much. After all, he was helping her by giving her shelter and safety from her father. And how could they freely walk the streets of Fort Worth without running into someone from her father's congregation?

"I shouldn't leave the house. Papa has men searching for me."

"I understand. So my driver will drop us at the back door of my dressmakers. She's been told to expect our arrival and her shop will be closed while we're there. You're going to receive your own private shopping spree."

Stunned, Rose sat back. "I should help pay for this."

"No," his mother said. "Once, I was in a similar situation as you. This is my way of repaying the universe for helping me to escape. Someday, you should do the same for another young woman."

The servant picked up her dishes.

"Now, don't tarry, we need to get going," she said. "And then I'm taking you back to the house. You and my son are going to have dinner with us tonight and you'll meet Hayden's sisters."

It was all too much. Tears trickled from her eyes. "Thank you for being so kind to me. I thought you would disapprove of me."

The woman grasped her hands. "No, dear. I'm thrilled for my son. When my son chooses a wife, I will accept her and love her and trust his judgement. But I'm still worried you're going to break his heart."

And that was a real possibility. As much as she cared for Hayden, her career was her gift from God, and she planned on pursuing that life if at all possible.

CHAPTER 12

*H*ayden knew better than to let his mother take Rose shopping, but she needed clothes and he didn't have time. But this afternoon, his mother had sent a message telling him that Rose was at their house meeting his sisters. Dinner would be held at six. *Your presence is expected.*

That gave him very little time to get Rose to the saloon before eight, before her father's men surrounded the place.

While he knew his mother meant well, she was putting them in grave danger of being exposed. Of Rose's father's men finding them.

When he arrived at the house, he could hear his sister playing the piano. Beth loved music, and he knew she would get along well with Rose.

As he walked through the door, the place was as usual in total chaos. The dog, an Irish Sitter, ran to him and jumped up and down on him before his sisters descended on him.

"Hayden," Cissie cried as she ran to him and launched herself into his arms.

"How is the brat?"

"They won't let me play baseball. The boys tell me that girls don't play baseball."

A chuckle escaped him as he thought of himself at her age and how he didn't want the girls to play either.

"I'm a good player. Mother won't interfere. She told me young ladies should learn needlework, but I don't want to do stitching. I want to hit the ball with the bat and be better than the boys."

"Then do it," he told her. "Get the ball and practice. Let the boys see how well you are doing and then they'll come to you."

She hugged him around the neck. "Thank you, Hayden."

He set her down and then proceeded to kiss each of the older girls on the cheek. It had been a month since he'd seen them and he missed all of them.

"We like Rose," Beth whispered in his ear. "She's been working with me on the piano. I've learned so much from her. Please tell me you'll bring her back."

"We'll see," he promised.

He glanced over and saw her sitting on the piano bench watching him. She smiled and then stood and twirled for him in a new dress that was elegant and beautiful. A grin spread across his face and she mouthed *thank you*.

With his sisters in tow, he walked to her side, leaned down and kissed her on the cheek. "You look beautiful," he said. "The shopping trip was a success?"

"Your mother made me buy way too much," she said. "I'm going to pay you back."

"If it makes you feel better. But not until you're a sensational opera star."

A blush spread across her cheek and she ducked her head

before glancing up at him. "Your mother knows how to spend money."

A laugh came from him and he saw his mother standing in the doorway watching them. Oh, how he wanted his family to approve of Rose. Even his father.

"She now has a fabulous wardrobe and you have a hefty bill from my dressmaker," she said with a smile. "Don't you think she looks beautiful."

"Yes. And that's what I expected," he said.

Rose blushed. "You shouldn't."

"But I wanted to," he said.

She smiled. "Beth has been practicing all afternoon with me. She's going to play you a song and I'm going to sing."

His sister grinned and sat on the piano bench. As soon as Rose opened her mouth to sing, his entire family stopped what they were doing and turned to stare. The sound of her voice reached deep in his chest and tugged at his heart.

His mother strolled over to his side and he glanced at her with a smile.

"You were right. She's got a beautiful voice. And I really like her."

"Me too, Mother," he said, watching the way her face animated with the song. How could he let her go when all he wanted to do was pick her up and carry her upstairs and have his way with her.

Not an appropriate thought with his family standing around.

When she finished, his father stepped out of the dining room. "The servants are ready to serve dinner."

"We're coming, Steward," his mother called.

Rose joined him and he kissed her on the cheek. "Beautiful."

"Thank you," she said as he took her hand and led her into the dining room.

They all traipsed around the table, finding their seats. Hayden noticed the way his father said nothing to Rose. His mother leaned over at the table and whispered in his ear, "I'm working on him. Give it time."

The normal chatter around the table occurred as they passed the plates of food. Hayden laughed and talked with his sisters like normal. Rose smiled and laughed with them, as well, while his father sat at the table like a bump on a log.

An ache grew in his chest at the way his father was treating the woman he cared so much for. It would be hard to forgive him if he didn't accept Rose.

After they were finished, his father pulled him aside. "In my office, now."

His sisters took Rose by the hand and led her back to the piano.

"Sing for us again," Cissie asked her.

Hayden followed his father into his study. His father poured him a brandy and they sat in soft leather chairs.

If the liquor was supposed to appease him, it wasn't working. Already, he felt angry toward his father for not even speaking to Rose.

Finally, the man sank into a chair.

"The girl is beautiful and has a wonderful voice," his father said.

"Yes," Hayden replied, not wanting to say more than was necessary.

They sipped from their drinks and then his father shook his head. "Her father is searching the town for her. Where is she staying?"

"She's safe," he said, not wanting to tell his father her location, because he feared the man would contact the reverend, even though he was known for disliking the preacher. But it would be one way he could separate them. Then Hayden would be available to marry someone else.

Someone of his father's choosing.

"I hope you're smart enough not to let her stay at your place. She is not the woman for you. This girl is going to be nothing but trouble."

With a sigh, Hayden didn't respond, not wanting to lie to his father, but unwilling to confirm his suspicions.

"Papa, how did you feel about mother when you met her?"

The man stopped and stared at his son. "Don't compare this woman to your mother. There is no comparison."

"Then answer my question. How did you know that mother was the woman for you?"

His father sipped from his crystal brandy glass and Hayden wondered at his reluctance. "We met at a party. It was back on the East Coast and the Vanderbilts were hosting a social I was invited to. The moment I saw her, I was struck by her beauty, her grace and elegance. I had to know more about her."

Hayden smiled. "Thank you. It was the same for me, Papa. The moment I saw Rose singing up on that stage. Her voice reached down inside my chest and twist me into knots. I didn't even know what she looked like because her face was hidden behind a veil."

There was silence.

Finally his father said, "It would be better if you were to meet and marry a socialite. Someone of your own social standing. Someone whose family has money."

This was what his father had been preaching since the time he turned twelve.

"Was mother a socialite? Someone of your social standing?"

His father stood and poured himself another drink. "No. She was not even invited to the party, but somehow managed to sneak in. All she wanted to do was see where the Vanderbilts lived. And then she met me."

Hayden glanced at his watch. It was after seven and Rose went on at eight.

"Would you change meeting Mother?"

"Absolutely not," his father said, glancing at him like he was crazy. "That woman has made a home, given me children, and supported me in every way. My life would never be complete without your mother."

"Then wish the same for me, Papa," he said, rising from the chair. "She may not be the socialite you wanted me to marry. But I'll be a lucky man if she were to marry me. Right now, I'm not even certain she would consider me. But the time I've spent with her convinces me more and more that she's who I want."

His father groaned. "But she's Reverend Tuttle's daughter and that man is a religious crackpot. You have an obligation to this family to marry someone of your social sphere. And Rose does not meet that criteria."

Hayden nodded. "Yes, but we can't choose our parents, or believe me, I think she would have found someone else."

"Do not expect me to accept her into this family. It will never work."

There was silence. Hayden was determined that he would not accept his father's words and if he wouldn't accept Rose, then basically they were done.

"No vows or promises have been made yet."

"Good. Don't do it. Somehow you must get rid of her."

Get rid of her? What did he want him to do, just drop her off in the middle of the street? Knowing his anger was about to explode, he gritted his teeth.

"I'm not getting rid of Rose. I'll protect her with my last breath. And no, I'm not going to marry some prim and proper society girl with a dowry. Change your plans."

His father's face turned red. "Hayden."

"I've got to go. She goes on at eight and it's going to be hell trying to sneak her in."

His father shook his head. "I don't like this. Not one bit."

"And I don't like your attitude," Hayden said as he walked out the door.

Rose was sitting with Beth on the piano giving her more instructions.

"We've got to go. It's after seven," he said.

She reached out and hugged Beth. "I'll be back and I'll show you even more."

"Please, oh, please," Beth said. "I can't wait."

Standing, she went over to his mother and hugged her. "Thank you for such a lovely day. I can't remember the last time I had so much fun."

"Come back, Rose," his mother said. "Just remember what we spoke about."

"I will," she whispered.

What had they talked about? Why had his mother thought that bringing her here was a good idea?

"Let's go," he said and held the door open for her.

CHAPTER 13

They were in his carriage headed toward the saloon. Rose had never had such a great time and she was envious of his family. Yes, she had a brother and a sister, but she had fallen in love with his many sisters. Especially Beth.

They shared a common love of music. And the young girl had been eager to learn more about the piano.

"What did you and my mother talk about?"

The man was fishing and he was worried, as he should be. But she would never tell him how his mother had told her about how she met his father. How she had been a poor young woman who tricked her way into the party where they met.

"Womanly stuff," she said smiling. "Nothing to concern yourself about."

"I doubt that," he said.

"What did you and your father talk about?"

His father had been rather cold toward Rose and she understood that she was not the kind of woman he wanted Hayden to be involved with. And were they involved?

He had kissed her that one time on the mouth and then

several times on the cheek or forehead. But the man had not made any moves on her that indicated he was interested, other than asking her to be his mistress.

And there was no chance of that happening.

The way he had backed off made her uncertain as to whether he was interested, though his mother assured her that he was most definitely attracted to her. More than he should be. But what were the signs?

If only her mother had told her more about what to expect from a man. But then maybe she didn't know since she married her father so young and quickly.

"Are you attracted to me?"

His head jerked around and even in the darkness, she could feel his eyes staring at her.

"Are you joking? Just because it's all I can do to keep my hands off of you. Last night, I couldn't sleep knowing you were down the hall, just doors away from me. Thinking of you lying in the bed, curled naked between the sheets. Ohhhh," he groaned.

She started to laugh.

"What's so funny? I don't see or feel any humor in this situation."

"I wasn't naked. I slept in my disguise."

"Do you think that matters? I would have gladly helped you remove them. But I promised not to try to sleep with you and I keep my word." He growled. "Oh, how I wish I had never given you my word."

She reached out and laid her hand on his arm. "You're the first man to show an interest in me. I don't know what happens between two people who are courting or seeing each other. And you must admit, our situation is a little weird."

Suddenly he pulled her against him and with his hand, he

tilted her face up to where she was staring in his eyes. "I know. And I didn't go about things the right way the first time, so I'm trying to do better. But here is a reminder of how I truly feel about you. How I can't stop thinking of you."

His mouth descended on hers, his lips demanding and controlling. His fingers reached up and held her face to where she couldn't move as he assaulted her lips. Fire spread through her like a raging heat storm in areas she'd never felt before. It was as if he wanted to crawl inside her as his tongue invaded her mouth, scorching her with his need.

"Sir, we've got trouble," his driver called.

They broke apart and she leaned back against the seat, her breathing labored and fast. What had he just done to her?

"What is it, George?"

"There is a mob standing around the White Elephant Saloon. They're checking everyone who goes in, sir."

"Drive on by," he said.

"What? No, I've got to go to work."

"You heard the driver, your father's men have surrounded the saloon."

"There must be a way that we can get in."

Hayden sank back onto the leather cushions. "Are you afraid of heights?"

"No, at least, I don't think so," she said, wondering if he meant for her to scale the building.

"George, take us down the back alley several buildings down. Far enough they can't see us."

She felt the carriage turn and soon they were heading down a darkened alley. The only reason she knew it was the alley was because there were no streetlamps and the road was bumpy as she bounced around on the seat.

How many times had she snuck down this alley to reach the saloon?

"What are we going to do?"

"We're going to see if O'Hara's will let us go up on their rooftop. Then we walk across the roofs until we reach the White Elephant Saloon. Hopefully, he will have some kind of door on the roof. If not, I don't know what we'll do."

The buildings were connected, but she'd never been on a roof before and she wondered at the safety.

"Thank God, they're flat roofs," she said as she touched her fingertips to her lips. She wanted him to continue kissing her. She wanted to experience more of what he did to her mouth, but she knew they were drawing close to the drop-off location.

"Tonight, if there is any problem at all, you get to me and I'll get you out of there."

While she knew he would do everything to protect her, she worried that with a mob of cowboys if that would be possible.

"I'm not afraid," she said. But then again, how far would her father go to get her back.

"Well, I'm nervous. Obviously, your father has learned that you're singing at the White Elephant."

"Yes, and that makes me sad. Because he will make certain that his congregation punishes Randal who has been nothing but kind to me."

"You're making him lots of money," he said. "That saloon used to be damn near empty every night."

She tilted her head. "Really? Why did you go there?"

The man sighed. "Sometimes, I get lonely. It was nice to sit and watch the cowboys get drunk. But all that changed when you started singing there."

She laid her head on his shoulder. "Thank you, Hayden. You've been a good friend."

"Friend? We are not friends. Understand that we will never be just friends. And if I had anything to say about this, we'd be lovers."

A giggle escaped her.

The very thought of them being lovers had her imagination going wild with images of the two of them naked, entwined in each other's arms.

"Maybe someday we will," she said almost taunting him.

He slammed her down on the seat and crawled on top of her. "Do not tease me. You're an innocent and not wise in the ways of a man. But just the thought of stripping your clothes off does this to me."

He pressed his erection between her legs and she gasped.

Just then the driver pulled the horses to a stop and set the brake.

Quickly before he could open the carriage door, Hayden sat up and pulled Rose up with him.

The door opened and he stepped out first. Stunned, she sat there realizing she'd just felt his cock between her legs. She made Hayden excited.

His arm reaching inside for her, she took his hand and stepped out and through the back door of the restaurant. Hayden spoke to a man and he pointed to a set of stairs in the back. Quickly, they hurried up the stairs.

The place was dusty and she could tell even in the darkness that few people came up here. A rat scurried in the shadows.

"Oh, dear," she said with a shudder as she hurried up the stairs. *Don't look*, she told her herself over and over. *Just follow him up the stairs.*

Hayden opened a door and they walked out onto the roof. Taking her by the hand, they walked carefully across the roofs of the connected buildings. When they neared the White Elephant Saloon, she could hear the men checking the customers who tried to enter the saloon.

"Take off your hat," one man hollered.

"They're checking to make certain you're not dressed as a man," Hayden said quietly.

"Remember, I was wearing men's clothing when my mother saw me last."

Randal came out of the saloon's front doors. "The sheriff has been notified. You're harassing my customers now go away. Rose is not here."

She watched as her father approached the owner of the saloon.

"We're not leaving," her father said. He pulled out his Bible and began to read a verse. His voice carried loud and clear. Right there in front of the saloon on the street, he began to preach.

"Maybe I should leave," Rose said. Maybe she should talk to Sadie about leaving Fort Worth, but how?

"Do you think he would come into the saloon?"

"Oh no, that's an evil place. The devil resides there and he's not stepping foot inside." How many times had he driven their wagon down the streets and told them of the perils of sin and evil that resided on this street?

"Then as soon as we get you inside, you'll be safe."

"Until my father gives up on me, I will never be safe," she said. "Why can't they just accept that I'm never marrying that man."

"Honey, I don't know, but over my dead body will you be his wife."

Her flesh tingled and she wondered if Hayden was meant to be her husband. But first, she had to learn if she could make it in New York. That had to be her focus.

And knowing her father, she feared he would force her to wed if he caught her. Killing Hayden would be ridding the world of one more sinner and rescuing his daughter. She could not be responsible for something happening to Hayden.

The very thought caused her heart to seize in her chest.

"Promise me you'll be careful."

He turned and glanced at her. "No one is going to get hurt. Now, come on," he said. "Let's get you inside."

As they walked across the roof, he found a door that led into the saloon. When she reached the dressing area, Randal came rushing over to her.

"How did you get in here?"

Hayden smiled. "The roof. We came through O'Hara's and walked across the building tops."

"Your father is not going to let you sing," he said. "They will storm the place."

"No, they won't," she said. "Your place is filled with the devil and sin. He's not coming in here for any reason."

Randal looked fearful. "If you're certain. The men are all here to hear you."

"Then let's give them the show they deserve."

CHAPTER 14

*R*andal let Hayden sit on the side of the stage. From there, he watched the crowd, looking for anyone that he feared would rush the stage. They had an agreement that if something went wrong, Hayden would scoop her up and get her back to the roof as soon as possible.

Sitting there, he watched the cowboys trying to flirt with her and how she ignored them, her focus on the music. Tonight, more than ever, her voice seemed to lift the rafters and he feared the roof flying off into the night.

Even the cowboys seemed to realize her voice was special. And after tonight, he feared she would not be singing in the saloon again. How could she?

As he watched her, he wondered how the woman could believe he wasn't interested in her. How could she not see that he wanted her enough that he was willing to fight his father over her. The crowd outside sounded even larger and an uneasy trickle of nerves scurried up Hayden's spine.

Halfway through her act, the door burst open and men poured through the doors of the saloon.

"Where is she? The preacher wants his daughter back," a man yelled, determined to reach the stage.

Hayden jumped up and grabbed her arm. They raced toward the stairs as fast as they could.

Fear pumped through his system as he heard the footsteps behind them.

"I never thought he would go to this extreme. I never believed he was capable of such," she said as Hayden pulled her up the last steps to the roof.

From below, he could hear the men screaming her name, looking for her. When they reached the door, he yanked it open and pulled her through. Then he found a piece of wood to wedge under the frame. Hopefully that would give them a little longer.

"Hurry," he told her as they ran across the roof in the darkness. When they reached O'Hara's, he could hear the men breaking down the door on the roof of the White Elephant.

When she turned to him, he saw the fear reflected on her face as he shoved her inside. They hurried down the stairs and out the back. But now the alley was filling with men.

"There she is," someone shouted.

His carriage came rolling up out of nowhere and he swore he was going to give George a bonus.

He yanked the door open and shoved her inside. Before he could get the door closed, his driver was hailing to the horses.

The carriage bounded through the alley bouncing along the uneven road.

With a sigh, he relaxed against the seat as the horses galloped down the darkened alley. If anyone stepped in front of them, they were a dead man walking.

"I can't do this anymore," she said. "He's going to hurt someone." She gazed up at him in the light from the passing streetlights; he could see she was terrified. "I'm so afraid it's going to be you who is injured. His parishioners would do anything he asked. I've got to return home."

"No," he said. "What's the one thing that would stop him from bothering you?"

"Me leaving," she said. "Then he couldn't find me."

"Oh no, as persistent as your father is, I think he would find you even in New York. He'd contact someone in the church there and the next thing you know, you'd be captured and returned to your father. What else would stop him?"

Surely, she knew what he was thinking. What he was going to offer her.

He watched as it dawned on her what would stop him. Probably the only thing.

"No, I want to live independently for a while. Why does it seem like all my life, someone has been in control of me? Even now, you're in control."

Shocked, he stared at her. Why had he never considered a woman's feelings before now? Did his sisters feel this need for independence? An urge to make their own decisions? How could he give Rose what she longed for and keep her safe?

With a sigh, he sat not knowing how to help her reach the conclusion that unless she wanted to return to her father, she needed to marry him. Now.

"Do you think you would be more independent with me or your father?"

"You, of course," she said. "It's just that I wanted to become a popular opera singer on my own. And then eventually marry a man who courts me. Raise a family and know that I was once a star."

At least they wanted many of the same things in life. A family. She didn't plan on singing in the opera for all her life.

Didn't she see that she needed him to help her reach her goals?

"What if I promised to take you to New York if you married me. To help you become the famous opera singer, as long as when you were done, we came back to Fort Worth and raised a family."

The sounds of horses following them alerted him that they were still not in the clear. If they could just reach his home, they could close the gates and be locked inside.

"Do you love me? I wanted to marry for love, not because my father found a man or you saved me from my father and promised me New York."

At first all he wanted to do was sleep with her, but now he realized that there was so much more with this woman that he longed to explore. No other woman intrigued him, like Rose. No other woman made him think of things like a home and family.

Yes, he loved her. But if he told her, she would never believe him. And yet, he would say those magical words right now, if she would hear them. But she still wasn't certain about him. And he didn't know how to convince her that he would make her happy.

He was a patient man and he would give her time. But he knew his feelings and they were more than just sex, they were forever.

"What I can offer you at the moment is I'm in awe of you. Will that become love, maybe. But I'm willing to take you to New York. Keep you safe and secure. I'm madly attracted to you, so much that my mother is worried about me."

Sitting in the carriage, he could see her contemplating his words. "Can you let me think about it? Maybe I can talk to my mother. Maybe she will convince my father that I'm never coming back to marry who my father chose."

Right now, she wasn't certain and he didn't know how to convince her that he would give her a good life. "As my wife, you will never want for anything. I'll take care of you and our family. But I do have one small requirement. When I marry you, there is no going back. No returning to your family or the church. And never expect that I will become a member of your father's congregation."

She nodded. "Just give me some time to think about everything."

Just then, they pulled into the drive and his men were there to close the gates behind them. They were safe for one more night. But how much longer could he keep her father away?

CHAPTER 15

*R*ose barely slept at all that night. It wasn't that she wasn't attracted to Hayden. She very much was, but marriage had been her dream of happily ever after. A man courting her, asking her father for her hand and getting down on one knee.

Instead, her father made the decision on his own without asking her what she thought. And now he had made her life so miserable, she was considering marrying a man she didn't love. There was a mutual attraction, but how did you make a marriage, especially a happy one, built on nothing but being drawn to a person.

And though her parents' marriage was strange, she wanted a marriage more like Hayden's parents. She'd so enjoyed spending time with them. Seeing how they cared for one another. Wishing she had the same kind of life. Yes, his father had been cold to her, but he was protecting his son.

How would he accept her if Hayden decided to marry her and she said yes? He wanted a debutante for his son, not a preacher's daughter. A woman known for singing in a saloon.

Knowing that Hayden would be gone, she rose from bed, dressed in one of her new gowns and went downstairs. If she married him, this would be their home, this would be her life. Was it what she wanted?

As she stepped into the kitchen, Hayden was sitting at the breakfast table.

"What are you still doing here? Don't you have to go to the office?"

Today, he looked especially handsome in a light blue shirt that brought out the color in his eyes. Yes, she was definitely drawn to him, but she had so little experience with men.

"Are you running me out of my own home?"

"Of course not, but usually you're gone by now."

He stood and pulled out her chair for her. Since their very first meeting, the man had always been so polite, a real gentleman. He treated women with respect.

The maid came in and poured her a cup of coffee. Oh how she could get used to this kind of life. But what about Hayden?

Did she love him?

"Today, you need to stay in the house and don't go near the windows. I'm coming home at lunch to check on you," he said. "I'm worried we were followed last night and that your father knows you're here."

If she ever had children, they would be allowed to make their own decisions regarding the partner they chose to marry. She took a sip of coffee.

"All right. Maybe I should go back to Sadie's place," she said.

"No, her home is not as protected as mine," he said. "There will be men at both places if your father is intent on capturing you. If something happens, George will show you to a hidden room. Go with him."

A hidden room. How intriguing. She almost wanted to find the space and check it out.

He rose from the table, walked over to her side, leaned down and kissed her softly on the lips. "Try to have a good day. Think about what we talked about last night."

"You haven't proposed," she said.

"And I'm not going to until I'm certain this is what you want. Remember, this would be my wedding as well. I want to do something special if and when I ever propose to you."

Her spirits soared at the thought of marrying Hayden and she smiled at him. "Thank you, I will think about it today."

There was so much to consider. This was when she needed to talk to her friends. "Do you mind if I send a note to Sadie and ask her to come speak to me?"

"Yes," he said. "Not because I don't like her, but I fear she's being followed. If she came here, they would know you were here for certain."

Why did the man have to be so smart? He was right. She knew he was right, but that didn't make it any easier. If only she could speak to Sadie and Tessa, they would help her make the right decision.

"All right," she said, wondering if it were possible for her to sneak out for just a little bit.

For a second, he paused. "Rose, I know that look. You're wondering if you could make it to her house. No, don't attempt it. They'll capture you."

"Oh, all right," she said with a snap.

"See you at lunch," he said as he walked out the door.

After he was gone, she finished her breakfast and went into the library looking for something to read. At home, she never had idle time on her hands, and yet here, she had nothing to do. No piano to practice on, nothing but wait.

Seeing the newspaper, she picked it up and carried it to a chair away from the window. Such a shame she couldn't open it and gaze out at the lovely yard. Listen to the birds sing and watch the bees pollinate the flowers.

Gazing through the pages, she stopped on the society page and was stunned to see her name.

Rumor has it that a certain young preacher's daughter has flown the coop and is singing down at a saloon on Main Street. When are these young women going to learn that a life on the stage is not proper and especially for a preacher's daughter? Another bad girl in town.

Last night, men were seen in the streets trying to locate her and she could be heard singing at the White Elephant Saloon. Maybe it's time for the city to clean up Hell's Half Acre. Maybe it's time for our mayor to shut down this sinful den where men drink and see a woman singing in an outfit that the local prostitutes probably loaned her.

That bitch!

It was all Rose could do to keep from jumping out of her chair and marching down to the newspaper and setting this woman straight. She never wore scantily clothed outfits, and in fact, dressed even more conservatively to keep them from gazing at her like a dog in heat. Betty Griffin was a snake in the grass. And now she was trying to make Rose her next victim.

When she continued reading, she squished the paper in her fists.

Now, there are rumors about her being with a very rich young man here in town. Are wedding bells about to ring or has our young woman become the man's mistress. When I learn the details, I'll let you know.

She was so furious, she jumped up from the chair and found the maid.

"I need a small gift box," she told her.

Sitting at the desk, she wrote:

Dear Mrs. Griffin,

I'm certain you like nothing better than to spread vile rumors about young women. But you're wrong. Dead wrong about me. I'm still as virginal as the day I was born. I'm a singer. And the saloon is the only opportunity for me to sing. I sing opera to these men, religious songs, and even ballads. No scantily clad clothing. No clandestine meetings with men. I'm no man's mistress. Can you say the same? Oh, and by the way, when and if I decide to marry, you'll be the last to know. Inside this gift box is what I think of you and your column.

Enjoy!

Rose

Yes, it was wrong. She knew it was wrong, but that woman had been publishing bullshit for so long, she needed some fresh manure. Disobeying Hayden's orders, she walked outside to the stables where the horses were kept. As soon as she walked in, George came to her.

"Miss you need to stay indoors. Mr. Lee would not like you being seen."

"Excuse me, George, but I need you to deliver a gift."

Taking a shovel, she scooped up some horse manure and carefully placed it in the box. Then she tied a very pretty bow on the outside.

"Please take this to Betty Griffin, along with this note."

"But, ma'am..."

"No, I don't want anyone else. I want Rose," he said, his anger rising. "Did your father pick out my mother?"

A frown crossed his father's face. "No."

"Well, I don't want you picking out my wife. Now we're done here. I'm going home to Rose since I know there is no real emergency. And don't expect me to respond the next time you insist there is an urgent matter and we need to discuss."

Like the snap of a bull whip, Hayden spun on his heel and left the hotel. Yes, he knew he'd left behind the woman his father had chosen for him, but he really didn't care.

There was no way he would even consider Helen Davis after she ran around with the one girl, who with Mrs. Griffin's help, liked to make everyone in town miserable. Nellie Robinson.

As he left the hotel, a sense of urgency overcame him. He needed to get home to Rose.

Though it wasn't dark yet, it soon would be.

CHAPTER 19

*R*ose heard someone pounding on the door. Careful not to let anyone see her, she peeked from behind the curtains to see who was knocking.

Shock radiated through her as fear seized her. There were five men standing on the front porch, including her father.

"Rose, I know you're in there. Come out now," her father demanded.

Suddenly she heard the maids squeal and knew that someone had entered the back of the house. How had they gotten through the gate?

"Who are you? Get out, now."

And she had sent George away just when she needed him the most.

Turning, she fled up the stairs. They were in the house. Where was the safe room that Hayden had mentioned? Why hadn't he showed her. Knowing they would search every room, she looked for a bedroom that had a balcony. Some way for her to escape and get away.

"Rose? Where are you?" A man shouted for her. "I'm going to find you."

Oh, why had she gone upstairs. If she'd gone into any other room downstairs, she might have been able to climb out a window.

Opening a door, she glanced in one of the empty bedrooms and saw a large trunk. She opened it, but it was filled with memorabilia from Hayden's college days.

The sound of footsteps on the stairs let her know she was running out of time. The bed frame was high and she crawled beneath it hoping the long bed skirt would hide her.

Doors were being opened and closed.

"Rose, I'm going to find you. Your papa is waiting downstairs."

Or course, he was. The man would not enter a building he considered evil and Hayden's home would certainly be possessed by the devil. If they found her, she would have to endure a cleansing ritual to rid her body of Satan's influences.

She shivered at the thought.

Footsteps were right outside her door. He threw open the door and she held her breath, waiting.

"Did you find her?"

"Not yet. Did you check all the rooms?"

"Yes. What if she's not here? We could be charged with breaking and entering. Trespassing."

The man laughed. "No, the Lord is on our side. Now go check every room, every closet again."

Shaking began to take hold of her as she knew they would eventually find her.

Suddenly a shout came from the back of the house.

"Get the hell out of my house."

Relief flooded her. It was Hayden. He was home. The man

slammed the door shut and hurried down the stairs. She could hear the other man running down the stairs.

Shouting was going on, but she couldn't understand the words. Slipping out from under the bed, she walked to the door and peeked out.

Hayden was watching as the sheriff handcuffed the two men. Did she dare go downstairs?

One of the maids must have contacted Hayden and the sheriff.

Finally, the sheriff hauled the two men out the door. But where was her father? Why wasn't he being arrested?

The sound of footsteps racing up the stairs had her shrinking back.

"Rose, where are you?"

With relief, she flung open the door and ran into Hayden's arms. Tears flowed down her cheeks. "Thank God, you're here. I was so afraid."

"Me too," he said. "How did they get in?"

"I don't know. My father was at the front door, but I pretended I wasn't here. Then I heard the maids screaming and that's when the man entered through the back door. After that, I don't know what happened, I was hiding under the bed."

For a moment, she stood there in his arms, feeling safe and cared for. Feeling like this was where she belonged.

He leaned back and his mouth covered hers and she relished the feel of his lips as they took control. The way they consumed her mouth. Passion began to spread through her and a craving built inside for something she didn't understand.

Hayden was the first man she'd ever kissed and she couldn't imagine doing this with any other man. She breathed in the scent of him and seemed to melt even more into his embrace.

Finally, they broke apart, but she didn't move. Didn't want to go anywhere, but to just remain in his arms safe and secure. What was she going to do? They could not continue to live this way. She had to either go back to her family and the church, give up her dreams and accept her life, or marry Hayden.

Hayden took her hand and led her into the bedroom where she had been hiding. As they sank down on the bed, he reached for her, running his hands down her arms. A rush of heat sent her blood raging through her. He put his hands around her waist and hauled her into his arms, molding her body against him.

Blood roared in Rose's ears as she leaned into Hayden's kiss, unable to resist the pull of his attraction any longer. The realization that she cared for this man had left her feeling reckless. What if he had been killed while trying to protect her? What if he had not come in time?

In his arms, she was defenseless against her unbearable need to feel the safety and protection of his embrace.

Consequences be damned, she was hungry for the feel of his body entwined around hers, delirious with wanting him, desperate to be possessed by Hayden. Yes, she was a virgin, but before she was forced to marry a man she hated, she wanted to be possessed by this man. His mouth plundered hers, and she returned his feverous kisses with a fierceness that surprised her.

She placed her hands on his face and molded his lips to hers, opening to receive him. He tasted of sun-kissed days and pleasure-filled nights. Sweet, sinful sensations erupted in a delicious soft moan that escaped from the back of her throat.

His hands gripped her shoulders as though he would never let her go, his lips plundering hers as he laid her back on the soft bed. Her body was flat against the surface as he leaned into his kiss, pressing his arousal through her skirts into the vee of her legs. From the feel of his muscular thighs to the strength of his sinewy chest, she felt all of him. Every delicious, rock-hard inch.

She slid her hands down his shoulders, down his muscled back, past his waist, until she gripped his buttocks, melding them even more firmly together against her. Right now, she needed him in a way she didn't understand, but she wanted to learn.

She was tired of fighting these sensations. She wanted Hayden, the man who rescued her, believed in her talent—and kissed like the devil.

He moaned, his tongue tracing the ridges of her lips, his kiss turning savage as she held him tightly against her, intoxicating her with desire. Nothing mattered at this moment except this man, this kiss and the feel of his body taut with need for her, only her.

Part of her mind refused to be quiet and warned her to step away, that it wasn't too late to stop this crazy risk she was taking with Hayden. But she knew she was past the point of control. Nothing could stop her from being with this man, not even the risk of losing her heart to him. Only he seemed to understand her. Value her and wanted her happiness.

Hayden made her feel alive; he made her feel things she tried to resist, and he made her feel like a woman. A woman deserving of love.

His lips moved to her throat, pushing the soft fabric of her dress out of the way as he slid his hands down the front of her dress, skimming her curves.

"Stop me now, or I'm lost," he said, his voice husky.

"No, only in your arms do I feel safe. Here is where I belong. Make me yours," she said, tugging on his shirt, pulling the material free of his pants, knowing a good girl would fight this temptation.

But it was like a fire raging inside her. And she no longer wanted to be a good girl. What had that gotten her?

She wanted to feel his naked flesh, run her fingertips over his muscles, down the wisps of hair on his solid chest. She wanted to touch him, make him as giddy with passion as she felt. She wanted Hayden, and she wanted him now.

At this moment, she needed to experience a man who had her best interest at heart. She was tired of fighting this thing between them; she was tired of denying the attraction she felt for him. And she feared what the future would hold after today.

With a final tug, his shirt came free of his pants, and she slipped her hands beneath the material, needing to feel his naked flesh. She ran her fingertips lightly up the hardened muscles of his chest, touching every solid ridge.

Why with Hayden just one smoldering glance and her senses were quivering with anticipation. Never had she experienced such temptation.

Rolling her on top of him, she leaned into every solid inch of him.

"Rose," he moaned, his lips covering hers once more. As their kiss deepened, his fingers deftly worked at the buttons on the back of her dress until she felt him sliding the sleeves over her shoulders, down her arms. Cool air brushed her skin, and she felt a moment of panic. What was she doing?

For God's sake, she was a virgin. Saving herself for her

husband. And then the image of the man her father wanted her to marry came to mind.

No, her mind screamed. Now, she must consummate with Hayden now. Before all was lost and she might never see him again.

And then his lips touched the sensuous part of her neck, causing her to shiver. Where were these feelings coming from? This need that consumed her. His lips trailed the material down her neck, nipping the curvature of her shoulder. A shudder went through her as his lips seared a path down her chest.

Rolling her over again, with a yank, her dress was removed and tossed onto the floor. Maybe she was crazy, but at this moment, nothing else mattered. Her breathing was fast and shallow as her fingers fumbled with the buttons on his shirt. Clumsily, she made her way down the front of the garment, resisting the urge to stop and let her fingers explore.

As she undid the last button, she yanked the shirt off of his back and tossed it to the floor with the other clothes. A shiver of need ran through her as she reached for the buttons on his pants.

There were no promises for tomorrow. There were no declarations of love. There was only this need to feel his arms around her. To let this man protect and love her.

"Wait, Rose," he whispered as he reached down and tugged his boots off, kicking them across the room. He stood, and she leapt from the bed and leaned into him. Not wanting the contact between them to end, she kissed his naked flesh, gently running her tongue along his chest, his skin rippling from the effect.

He grabbed her shoulders and pushed her back against the wall. Quickly, he untied the front of her chemise and pulled the cotton garment over her head, throwing the material in a haphazard way. She stood before him, bare from the waist up.

"You're so beautiful," he said, staring at her breasts.

Leaning up, she kissed Hayden, needing his embrace, unable to bear their bodies being separated. Her lips expressed what her heart knew and her voice could not say as he pulled the string on her drawers. They dropped to her feet, leaving her naked and exposed. He stepped out of her kiss, his eyes raking her with a warmth that was visible even in the dim light. Suddenly, standing there naked before him, all the doubts she had held at bay slammed into her with the realization they had promised each other nothing.

Maybe she worried too much, but the feel of his lips covering hers pushed aside her remaining doubts. There were no promises, but there was the pleasure of the evening.

Reluctantly, he released her lips, and she felt bereft at the loss of pleasure. He stepped out of her embrace and quickly finished unbuttoning his pants, shucking them and tossing the unwanted garment to the floor.

He stood naked, all male before her. His manhood protruded before him, smooth and long and hard. Sunlight streamed through the window and cast a glow about him. Was she falling in love with him? Could she be the wife he deserved and wanted?

With a cry, she reached out and touched his face, her hand caressing his cheek and pulling him toward her. "Hayden."

His lips covered her mouth as he backed her toward the bed. She felt the wooden frame touch the backs of her legs and found herself being laid gently on the bed. The mattress sagged when he joined her, and she knew soon she would give herself to him. Soon she would no longer be a virgin.

"Anything you want or need, I'm yours," he whispered, nipping the curvature of her neck.

At this moment, she didn't understand what she needed. All she knew was that this felt right. This was where she belonged.

His lips trailed down until he reached her breasts, and his mouth closed over her nipple, laving the bud until she gripped his head, her breathing harsh.

What kind of sensation was this? One that nearly drove her crazy with need.

His hands skimmed her body, sending shivers through her while his fingers delved into the soft curls that covered her femininity. She jerked at the unexpected jolt of pleasure that rippled through her. Only Hayden seemed to make her act like a wanton. Only he could break down her barriers and release the lustful woman inside. She wanted him desperately, yet she was afraid.

Rose moaned, the sound loud and voracious in the room. She arched against his hand, gripping the sheets against the raging need his hand was building with his caresses.

"Hayden!" she cried, as she tensed, trying to hold on to the sweeping pleasure that ascended on her as she disintegrated beneath his hand.

What had just happened? For a moment, she lay there, her breathing shallow and fast, her eyes closed while she slowly collected herself.

"Now I'm going to take your virginity," he whispered softly. "It may sting, but know that soon, the pain will be gone forever."

A whimper escaped her. After such pleasure, how could there be pain?

The feel of Hayden thoroughly aroused, spreading her legs, caught her attention.

She opened her eyes and gazed at him, his eyes dark, hungry, and so beautiful, she had to resist the urge to kiss each one.

She didn't want to love him, didn't want to experience these emotions. But there was no denying he made her feel wonderful. He made her laugh, he protected her, but most of all, he made her feel so alive. And there was no denying she was falling for him.

"Rose," he whispered, his husky voice sending tremors down her spine. "It's past time for me to feel you wrapped around me."

His knees nudged open her thighs, his hands gripped her waist as he brought her hips up to meet him and slowly he entered her until he met the wall of resistance. With a gentle shove, Rose felt the membrane break.

"Oh," she cried as she held onto him tightly at the wash of pain.

"It's over, and in a moment, the pleasure will begin."

She lay beneath him still as the ache slowly subsided. With a groan, the urge to lift her hips overwhelmed her and he responded by moving inside her. Joined as one, she gazed up into his lust filled eyes. This was as old as time and now she knew the meaning of life. She moaned as he thrust into her welcoming body.

"Hayden," she cried, unable to contain the passion their bodies were creating.

"Do you want me to stop?" he asked, staring at her, his gaze hard and unwavering.

"No, please no," she said, as she rose to meet each thrust.

He delved into her rhythmically, filling her, melding her to him while she clutched him, relishing in the feel of his flesh to hers.

With each recurring movement, his moans filled someplace deep within her heart. Sweat glistened on his brow, and Rose reached up to caress his face with her hand. He opened his eyes, staring at her, filling her soul as well as her body with sweetness, with a contentment that had long been denied. A pleasure that even now was rushing toward her, unstoppable.

Rose moaned with satisfaction as her body went rigid, spasms of desire surrounding Hayden. Cascading shivers of delight left her clinging to this man who was claiming her heart while he reached his own climax, shuddering, gripping her, as he found pleasure.

Rose breathed deeply the musky scent of Hayden and pressed her lips to the inside of his neck between gasps for air. She was completely spent as she lay relaxed, sated, and more confused than ever by the sensations Hayden seemed to generate.

Because she had given herself to his man, did that mean she loved him? Her heart was full at the moment and she cared so much, but was it love?

And what about her dreams of being an opera singer? What would this do to them?

CHAPTER 20

*H*ayden was filled with such pleasure as he lay next to the woman he loved. Now there was no doubt in his mind that they should marry. Even now, a child could be growing in her womb and while he would help her realize her dreams, he also would protect and love her and any children they created.

Their breathing had slowed as he rolled toward her and pulled her into his embrace. "Thank you."

"For what?"

"For making my dreams come true. I've thought of this moment for months and it was even better than I anticipated."

This evening, finding her frightened and in fear of her life, they had clung to one another. Now he knew with certainty that she was right for him. That she probably loved him but had yet to realize her feelings. At least he hoped so.

"Really?" she said. "I couldn't imagine."

"That's because you're a woman. Men think of sex often. But what just happened between us was more than I could ever predict."

It was so much better than what had kept him awake at night as he lay in his bed thinking of Rose. Now if only she would agree to marry him and they could somehow make her father realize that she would never go back to him.

The setting sun danced through the curtains and he wondered if even now her father had someone waiting outside for them. Today had frightened him so badly and driven her into his arms.

And though he had no doubts about proposing to her, he still had some qualms that she would put him before her career. Not that he didn't want her to be successful, but he needed to know that she loved him. That he was important to her.

As she lay in his arms, he wondered how he could propose to her. All he wanted to do now was take her down to the county clerk's office and marry her.

"Tell me what you would expect in a marriage. Are you willing to help me achieve my dreams or would I have to give that up?"

Hayden laced his hand through hers, loving the way they were lying side by side with the afternoon waning. "As my wife, your dreams would be important. But as your husband, I would expect to come first. I'm not saying we won't go to New York. I'm not saying that you can't be a star. What I'm saying is that at the end of the day, I expect you to love and want me more than your career."

Wasn't that what every man or woman wanted from their relationship? Someone who put them first above everything else?

"But you would ever stop me from singing?"

"Never, because I love to hear your voice."

She smiled and reached up and caressed his face. "You realize that my parents' marriage was all about my mother being subservient to my father. That all of us had to bow down to the fact that he was the leader of the family. I don't see that in your family. Would you expect me to be inferior to you?"

The idea of his mother being submissive to his father had a chuckle rising in his throat. She would kill his father before she bowed down to him. And that was one of the many traits he adored about his mother. But his father...their relationship was complicated.

So much was expected of the first and only born son.

"No, in fact, I want a partner. I have servants and I would never want my wife to answer to my beck and call. When it comes to our family, we make decisions together. These are both of our lives and each of us must be happy."

With a sigh, she gazed into his sapphire eyes. "Will you be patient with me while I learn to be the wife you want?"

A grin spread across his face. "If you'll be patient with me while I learn to accept that you're going to be a big star someday. That I will have to share you with the world."

A sigh of contentment escaped from her throat.

Naked, Hayden slipped from the bed, removing his arms from around her. She turned and gazed at him, her brunette hair spilling down around her shoulders, her dark eyes questioning him as she rose on her elbows curious as to what he was doing. He dropped to one knee. "Rose Tuttle, will you be my wife. Will you honor me by taking my hand and walking through life with me until death do us part?"

With a laugh, she threw her head back. "You're naked. You're proposing to me after we had sex?"

"Why not," he said. "I couldn't wait any longer."

It was true. For her safety, he knew she needed his name. His protection. But she also had his heart.

A grin spread across her face and she reached out and brought his lips to hers.

"Yes, oh, yes," she said against his mouth. "The sooner the better."

CHAPTER 21

*A*s Hayden was preparing to leave the house the next morning, Rose stood in the hallway gazing at him with anxious dark eyes. If only he could stay here with her, but he had to prepare their wedding.

"Don't leave the house. I've instructed the servants to make certain the doors remain shut and locked. Plus, I hired two extra security men."

She nodded. "This is ridiculous, me being afraid of my own father."

What could he say? He'd never known that Reverend Tuttle's church was so exclusive and determined that their women followed their laws. In some ways, it was frightening.

"After I go to the office, then I'm going to my parents to arrange the details of the wedding with my family," he said. "I'll be home before dark. And no, we're not going back to the White Elephant Saloon."

With a sigh, she nodded. "You're right. Someone will get hurt if I try to sing there again."

"Save your voice for New York," he promised her.

She reached up and kissed him. "Be careful. I know they're still out there."

He smiled. Her worrying about him made him feel good and showed she was starting to care for him.

The memory of how he had found men in his house when he returned home almost had him staying, but if they were to marry, he needed his family's help. Though he wondered how his father would react.

With one last kiss, he turned and fled out the door.

As he rode his horse through the gates of his home, he worried if he was making a mistake. Riding away, he looked for anyone who might be watching his house. The sheriff seemed to have gotten rid of them, and after he arrived at his office in downtown Fort Worth, he got busy managing the books of his father's company and paying the bills.

After his father's attempt at matchmaking how would he feel about Hayden leaving? Sure, he had enough money of his own, but being the only son, his father wanted him running his business. And he would soon be disappointed to learn that they were leaving for New York. As soon as they were married.

And would his father finally accept that he was marrying Rose. Not Helen or anyone else he tried to arrange a marriage for him with.

At four o'clock, he hurried out of the office and to his parents' home.

When his youngest sister, Cissie, opened the door, she flew into his arms. He hugged and twirled her around, knowing that soon, she would be too big for him to hold. It was only a matter of time.

"Is Mom and Papa around?"

"Yes," she said. "Did you bring Rose?"

"No, I did not," he said, not wanting his sisters to know of her staying at his home.

"Come in. They're out in the garden," she said.

When they walked out onto the patio area, he noticed that his father was reading the newspaper and his mother was knitting.

"Son, I'm so glad you're here. Did you bring Rose?"

"No," he said. "I need to speak with both of you."

His father laid down his paper and his mother her knitting needles.

A grin spread across her face. His mother always had an uncanny way of knowing something about her children before they told her.

"I asked Rose to marry me and she said yes."

His mother jumped up and ran over and hugged him. "I'm so happy for you, son."

His father continued to sit, staring at him, obviously displeased.

Shaking his head, he said, "Are you certain you're willing to put up with Reverend Tuttle the rest of your life? Eventually, I'm sure she will make up with her family. They will want to see their grandchildren. Can you stand that man after everything he's done? Helen Davis is a fine young woman who doesn't have all these problems."

No doubt about it, accepting Reverend Tuttle would be difficult. But if that made Rose happy, then he would clench his teeth and do his best to accept the man. Though he would never leave him alone with his children. A fear of how he would either steal or try to warp their brains with his crazy religion.

"Helen Davis is a mean girl. A woman who involves herself

with mean spirited women. I am not in the least attracted to her."

"Then we'll find you someone else. Anyone besides the Reverend Tuttle's daughter."

"No, Father," he said. "I'm marrying Rose."

"I was really hoping you would come to your senses."

His mother sank back down in her chair. "Our son is marrying a delightful young woman. Be happy for him."

At least his mother appreciated his choice. And his sisters already loved her.

"How can I when I know the next thing out of his mouth is that he'll be going to New York." The man stood and began to pace the patio area. "You can't up and leave."

Hayden did not deny that was their plans.

"Who is going to take care of the business while you're gone? This is a family run operation based right here in Fort Worth. You're the heir apparent and you're going off and leaving everything behind that I've entrusted you with."

How could he deny his father? It was true that he had given him free rein over his business and Hayden had made a fortune.

"It won't be for long or at least I hope not," he said. "But we've got to get away from her father."

He told them of how he came home and found Rose hiding beneath a bed and the men going through his house searching for her.

"It's bad enough that she's Reverend Tuttle's daughter, but for her to take you away from the family business is a deal breaker for me. Find someone else."

His father raised his paper as if the discussion was over.

Stunned, Hayden stood. "You've always encouraged me. Yes, I knew you would be disappointed, but I came here excited to tell you my news and ask you to host the wedding in the backyard. Instead, I learn you don't want me to marry her."

His mother jerked to glance at her husband. "No, son, I support your decision. There has to be some way we can work this out. We're the largest railroad in Texas, but surely the company could purchase a railroad in New York and you could run both businesses."

"Our main office is here in Fort Worth," his father said. "The head of the finance department needs to be here, not in New York."

Quietness descended over them.

"I best be going," Hayden said. "I've been gone all day and I fear something happening while I'm gone."

His mother rose and gave his father a glare. "I'll walk you to the door, son."

As they left the patio area and walked through the house, his mother put her arm around his. "Give me a day. You are the first of our children to move away and your father is upset. With my help, he'll come around. As long as you're happy, I'm thrilled."

They stopped in front of the door. "I'm nervous. My biggest fear is that she won't love me as much as she loves her career. This has been her dream for so long and if I didn't agree to this, she wouldn't marry me."

His mother reached up and kissed him on the cheek. "Son, things will change after you're married. If she loves you, then her priorities may change. Give it some time."

"That's the thing, we don't have time. The reason she agreed to marry me is to stop her father from getting her. Yesterday, he almost succeeded. And yet, I love her so much, I can't imagine my life without her."

A grin spread across her face. "What kind of wedding should I be planning?"

"A simple affair with the family and the local justice of the peace. Nothing extravagant. And it needs to be done as soon as possible."

"I'll get to work on it. Let's plan it for day after tomorrow," she said smiling. "Leave your father to me. I'll work on him."

CHAPTER 22

*T*hat night when Hayden got home, it was already dark. He asked his cook to make him a picnic basket.

"But, sir, it's dark. Is this for tomorrow?"

"No, it's for now."

With a smile, he found Rose sitting in his library reading a book.

"Hayden," she said with a smile. "I've been worried about you."

"Sorry, but I went to speak to my parents about the wedding. I think we should celebrate with a picnic. Out under the stars."

A frown furrowed her brow. "Is it safe?"

"Of course," he said as he took her hand and pulled her up. "Come on."

With a giggle, she followed him into the kitchen. The cook was just finishing up their basket. "Here, sir."

"Thank you," he said and was pleased to see she had found him a blanket to throw on the grass.

Taking Rose by the hand, he led her out the back door. The moon was shining bright and a cool breeze blew the scent of the gardenia tree next to the house.

She took the blanket from his arms and spread it on the ground.

"I've never been to a picnic at night."

"There are a lot fewer bugs," he said.

Sitting the picnic basket on the ground, he helped her sit and then plopped down beside her.

"We haven't had any time to talk today and I thought this might be a good place for us to have some privacy."

She licked her lips and glanced around nervously. "As long as you don't think my father's men will find us."

That had been a concern, but surely even God fearing men went to bed. They were protected and if there was a sign of trouble, they had plenty of time to get inside.

"We're all locked in behind the gates. The men are taking turns watching the house for any signs of trouble."

With a nod, she opened the basket. "Oh, cold fried chicken. My favorite."

"Mine too," he said.

For a few minutes, they ate the chicken in silence. When they finished, Hayden lay back on the blanket and looked up at the heavens. With a sigh, she put everything back into the basket and lay beside him.

"The stars are beautiful tonight."

"Yes," he said softly, wondering what they would look like in New York.

If at all possible, Hayden did not want Rose to know about his father's reaction to his wedding announcement. All it would take was some time and he was certain his father would love Rose as much as he did, but for now, it was better if she didn't know.

"Today, I spoke to my parents about us marrying day after tomorrow."

Rose leaned up on one elbow and gazed down into his eyes. "What did they say? Were they all right with us marrying so soon?"

He gave a chuckle. "Are you joking? My mother immediately began making plans. I asked her to keep it simple with just a few close friends and family with the justice of the peace marrying us in the garden. Is that all right?"

Rose gave a little laugh. "It sounds lovely. Day after tomorrow? Oh my, I don't have a dress."

A smile crossed Hayden's face. "Is it all right if Levi stands up with me?"

"Of course," she said. "But I'm worried about the right dress."

"I'll take you to the dressmaker's tomorrow."

"No, it's bad luck to see the bride in her gown before the ceremony."

"Well, you're not going alone."

She reached over and laid her lips on his. "I'm only doing this once and even though our wedding is rushed, I want it to be perfect."

Only a woman who cared would want her wedding to be perfect. Maybe she was falling in love with him. Maybe this wedding was not a mistake.

Pulling her down on top of him, he grinned. "We'll get you to the dressmakers somehow tomorrow."

She stared down at him and smiled. "When are we leaving for New York?"

"Right after the ceremony. We're on the next train out of town. This way we can get away from your family."

She nodded. "I'm going to miss Fort Worth and my friends, but we'll be starting a new life together."

A new life that Hayden had no idea what to do with in New York. He was considering purchasing another railroad. One that traveled across the continental United States. But he would have to wait and see if the opportunity was there.

She shifted to his side, her head lying on his chest.

"Tell me what you think our life in New York will be like."

"We'll rent an apartment, and after we're settled, you will start auditioning. During the day, you'll be working and I'll be looking at investments. Eventually, you'll get a part in the opera and I'll find something to keep me busy. At night, you'll come home to me and we'll talk about our days and make love into the night."

She sighed and gazed up at the stars. "What if I don't succeed? What if I'm a total failure?"

He laughed. "Honey, I've heard you sing. I've no doubt in my mind that you're going to be very successful."

She gave him a squeeze. "You always have faith in me and that makes me very happy."

"And I always will."

Now if they could just get through the next few days without another incident involving her father and his. The man was absolutely set on finding him a proper wife, but Hayden only wanted Rose. No one else.

Rising, he reached over and his mouth descended on hers as he claimed her lips, knowing that soon she would be his forever.

When they broke apart, he pulled her to her feet and

stood. "We've got a big day tomorrow. Buying a wedding dress and packing for New York. Soon you'll be Rose Lee."

In the moonlight, he saw a smile cross her face. Maybe she did love him after all. He hoped so.

CHAPTER 23

*A*fter much persuasion, Hayden finally agreed to let her go to a dress shop and purchase a wedding dress as long as he was nearby in case she needed him.

They pulled the carriage into the alley behind the shop and then he ushered her in. At the backdoor, she turned and gave him a quick kiss.

"Now you must leave. It's not good for the groom to see the bride in her wedding dress before the ceremony."

"No, I'm staying," he said.

"Then you can wait outside in the carriage. But not here in the dressmaker's shop."

A sigh escaped him. "All right, but you scream if you need me. I'll be sitting out here waiting for you."

She grinned. "Thank you. See you soon."

He glanced up at the dressmaker. "If there's trouble, you know where I'll be. And please do not let her pay for the gown. Put it on my tab."

"Hayden, no," Rose cried.

The lady grinned. "Yes, sir. We'll take good care of her."

With a smile, Hayden turned and went back out the back door.

Rose shook her head. He was much too generous. Funny that the single man had a tab.

The dressmaker put her in a private room and when she opened the door, there was Sadie trying on a wedding gown.

"Sadie," she screamed and ran to her. "Oh, how I've missed you so much."

The two women threw their arms around each other crying.

"Levi and Hayden set this up so that we could shop for our wedding dresses together," Sadie told her.

Tears welled in Rose's eyes as joy filled her at how considerate her husband-to-be was of her feelings.

"We've been so worried about you. Levi has been telling me about what your father has done. Oh, Rose, I'm so thrilled that you're marrying Hayden. Are you madly in love with him?"

She sighed and the two women sank down onto the chairs in the dressing room. "I'm not certain I know what love is. But I care about him deeply. He's kind and generous and he's so protective of me."

Sadie grinned at her. "Do your knees go weak when you see him and is he all you can think about?"

A laugh bubbled up from Rose. "Yes."

"You are falling in love, my friend."

Just then the door opened and the dressmaker walked in. "Ladies, here are some gowns for you to try on. Miss King, your wedding is months away, so if you don't like these, we can always design one for you. Miss Tuttle, you will have to choose one of these. We can make minor alterations."

The woman turned and left them and the two women jumped up and down. "We're getting married."

Finally, they stopped and laughed. "It's so great to see you. Let's try on wedding gowns."

For the next hour, the two women laughed and giggled as they put on the different dresses, finally choosing a simple gown in white satin and lace for Rose.

"It's too expensive, Sadie. Let me choose the cotton one."

"No," Sadie told her. "This dress is beautiful on you. It's perfect and meant to be your wedding gown."

"But Hayden has already done so much for me, I don't want to cost him anymore money," she said quietly.

Sadie took her by the hand. "Look, the man has enough money and he wants you to be happy. If you don't buy it, then I'm going to and send it over to you."

Oh, how she wanted to look perfect for Hayden. She longed for the approval of his family and to be accepted as one of them. If this dress helped her to obtain that status, then she would gladly buy it.

Rose shook her head. "Is it too fancy for a garden wedding?"

"No, it's not."

It suddenly occurred to her that she had no one to be her bridesmaid. Sadie had been her best friend since grade school.

"Would you please stand by my side when I marry Hayden," Rose asked.

A grin spread across her friend's face. "Of course, I will."

"We're getting married tomorrow in his parents' garden."

A frown crossed Sadie's face. "But Levi said his father wasn't happy about this marriage. Did he change his mind? Said he was upset about Hayden leaving for New York."

Stunned, it was the first Rose had heard about his father

not accepting her. Sadness filled her and she plopped onto a chair.

"Hayden hasn't said anything."

His family meant so much to him. She couldn't come between them. His father had entrusted him with the company and she would be taking him away from the railroad.

But she couldn't stay here. She had to get away.

Her friend looked confused. "Maybe I misunderstood." Sadie bit her lip and glanced away.

"Right after the ceremony, we plan to leave for New York. But Hayden didn't say anything about his father not approving. In fact, we have to get out of town or my father and the men of his church will do everything they can to keep us apart."

Sadie shook her head. "I'm sure I just misunderstood. Because his parents wouldn't be holding a ceremony in their yard if they didn't approve. Don't listen to me. Now come, let's get dressed and pick out some accessories to go with your gown."

The women hurriedly dressed, and laughing, they stepped out of the dressing room they had been sharing. Stunned, Rose and Sadie stared at Nellie Robinson and her crew of mean girls.

"Rose, I thought everyone at your father's church was searching for you," she said with a wicked smile that sent a cold trickle down Rose's spine. Of all the women to run into, Nellie was the worst.

"Oh, no, we settled that," Rose said, lying.

"That looks like a wedding gown in your hands. Are you getting married?"

Sadie stepped toward the woman. "It's my dress, Nellie.

Rose is just being kind to carry it for me while we shop for accessories."

The three mean girls all exchanged glances.

"Funny, I thought I heard something about you getting married tomorrow in a garden. Who are you marrying, Rose?" Nellie said with a grin. "Do you have to marry? After all I heard you were singing in a saloon."

The girls giggled.

"No, Nellie, I don't have to marry. I'm still as virginal as I've been since birth," Rose retorted, anger spiking through her. That damn article in the paper.

Nervous and not certain on how to get out of this, Rose resisted the urge to punch her. "Sadie is the one engaged to Levi. Me, I'm about to leave town and go to New York, so you don't have to worry about me stealing a man from you."

Just then the dressmaker came out and took the dress from Rose. "Should I put this on Mr. Lee's account?"

Why couldn't the woman just do what she'd been told? A snicker came from the mean girls.

"Hayden Lee?" Nellie asked laughing. "Boy, have you come up in this world. The most eligible bachelor in Fort Worth since Levi was taken by Sadie."

Rose lifted her chin and smiled. "Yes, Hayden Lee."

Sadie stepped in front of Nellie. "Rose is in a lot of danger. If her father finds out, they will take her away and marry her to a preacher from some Podunk town. Prove to me that you've changed. Show me that you've learned from your mistakes and keep this to yourself."

A smile flitted across Nellie's face. "Sadie, of course, I'm a different person since you took Levi away from me. I'm one of the good girls. Not a bad girl like the two of you."

Rose laid her hand on Sadie's arm. "Come on, Sadie, let's finish our shopping and go."

The three women turned to leave. "Happy wedding day, Rose," Nellie said and then they walked out the door.

After they were gone, Rose grew nervous. "What if she tells my father? What if they interrupt our ceremony? I would be so humiliated. Oh, Sadie, what am I going to do?"

Sadie hugged her friend. "Everything is going to be all right. Our men will have extra guards at the house and you're going to marry Hayden Lee. The two of you are meant to be together."

Before, Rose had not been nervous. But now she felt terrified. Of all people, why had she run into Nellie today.

CHAPTER 24

*N*ellie marched down the street, her anger showing with every step as she went toward the church. How dare that bitch Sadie say that to her. She never made a single mistake, except for making certain that Sadie had to march through town naked. Then she would not have stolen Levi from her.

As for Rose Tuttle marrying the richest man in town, it infuriated her. Rose needed to go back to her weird congregation and stay with her own people.

And Nellie Robinson was just the person to help her get back there. She wasn't about to keep this information to herself.

Hayden Lee needed rescuing from a disastrous wedding, one she was sure he would regret. And she was just the person to free him. And maybe even catch his eye in the process.

She stepped up to the church and knocked on the reverend's office. The door swung open and Mrs. Tuttle, who always looked like a drab little mouse, stood there in her gray clothes, her face pale.

"Hello, Nellie, what can I do for you?"

"I'm here to tell you about your daughter Rose," she said with a smile. "I know how you can bring her home."

Mrs. Tuttle swung the door open wider. "Please come in, Nellie. I'm sure my husband would love to talk with you."

A grin spread across Nellie's face as she stepped into the reverend's ugly office.

CHAPTER 25

*H*ayden was hiding in his bedroom, trying to pack his clothes and prepare for their trip to New York. He'd spoken at length with his mother this afternoon and the wedding arrangements were all made.

Only his father was still unaccepting of his marrying Rose and going to New York. Hayden wasn't certain that he would even be at the wedding, but his mother assured him his father would be in attendance.

Only question—would he be there willingly? Would he accept Rose and their decision for them to travel to New York? Time would tell, and right now, all Hayden cared about was making certain that Rose was safe until they said their vows.

A knock sounded on his bedroom door. "Who is it?"

"It's me," Rose said, her voice making him long to go to her.

"It's bad luck for us to see each other before the wedding," he said.

"I know, but I need an answer," she said.

What had caused her to suddenly have doubts?

Afraid that she was going to back out, he went to the door, but did not open it. He slid to the floor.

"Let's talk through the door," he said to her. "I'm sitting on the floor."

He heard her dress moving. "My hand is on the frame," she said. "It's my way of reaching out to you."

A smile flitted across his face. "My hand is touching yours through the wood. What's wrong, Rose?"

There was a sigh and then she said the words he didn't want her to know until after the wedding. "Does your father not want you to marry me and for us to move to New York?"

He couldn't lie to her because that would not be right, and yet, he didn't want to tell her the truth either.

"My father doesn't want his only son, the man who runs the family business, to go to New York. You're the person who is causing that to happen, so his solution is for me not to marry you."

Hopefully by breaking it down, she would realize that it wasn't so much about her, but the decisions they were making. Though deep down, Hayden also realized his father still had dreams of him marrying an heiress.

That would never happen.

It was quiet on the other side of the door and part of him wanted to jump up, throw open the barrier and take her in his arms. But that couldn't happen. They needed all the luck they could get. The wedding was in fewer than twenty-four hours, but already he'd doubled the security around the house and hired them to be at the wedding.

"Are you trying to tell me that it's more about you leaving the business than me?"

"Exactly. I'm his only son, the heir to the business, and

now I'm going to New York with my lovely bride. He's afraid we'll never return."

Again, there was a long spell of silence.

"Maybe you shouldn't marry me. I'm bad luck. You've done so much for me and your family is kind. We should call the wedding off and that way your father would be happy and mine would be ecstatic that I came home to him."

Now, she was scaring him. Terrified that she was going to back out, he had to somehow convince her that was a horrible idea.

"But that's not what I want. Rose, from the moment I laid eyes on you singing in the White Elephant Saloon, I've loved you. Yes, I messed up the night we first spoke, but even then, I wasn't certain my father would accept you. And he hasn't, yet, but I don't care. You are what I want and that's all that matters. I love you and want to spend the rest of my life with you. Right now, you're still finding your way, but I hope and pray someday you will love me."

On the other side of the door, he could hear her crying.

"I don't know what love is," she whispered softly. "I'm not certain that I've ever experienced it in my life."

Leaning his head against the door, he sighed. "I'm in no hurry. You know what I want in a wife. We've talked about it. I'm anxious to begin our life together. And I can't wait for us to get on that train headed for New York. We'll be back here eventually, but that time in New York is going to be our time. Our honeymoon."

She sniffled. "I think we've already started the honeymoon."

He laughed. "Do you know how hard it is for me to stay on this side of this door and not come out and carry you to my bed?"

"As hard as it is for me to stay on this side of the door?"

Heat coursed in his veins. He was certain she loved him, and soon she would tell him, but until then, he could wait.

"Tomorrow night, Mrs. Lee, I'm going to give you a wedding night like no one has ever experienced before. Don't plan on sleeping."

She giggled and then grew quiet. "Seriously, Hayden, if you think you need to call off this wedding to please your father, it's all right."

Sometimes his father could be the biggest pain that ever walked the planet. No, that was her father.

"You know we both have fathers who are controlling and demanding. We share that in common."

A gasp came from the other side of the door. "You're right."

"We're adults. We've made our decision. I'm not backing out of this wedding. Do you hear me?"

"Yes, Hayden."

"Are you going to back out?"

"No," she said and a smile crossed his face. This time she sounded strong. This time he felt certain that tomorrow night they would be married.

"Now, you need to go to bed and get some rest. Because tomorrow night you won't be sleeping," he said.

A rustle on the other side of the door let him know she was standing.

"Hayden, thank you for everything you've done for me. For loving me and making me happy. We're going to have so much fun in New York. I'm happy you're going with me."

A grin spread across his face as he heard her skirts swishing down the hall. Tomorrow was his wedding day and he couldn't wait.

CHAPTER 26

*H*ayden woke early the next morning and realized he hadn't bought Rose a wedding ring. Jumping up out of bed, he hurriedly dressed.

He rushed down the stairs and hurried out to the stable. Quickly, he saddled his horse. It was his wedding day and he was so excited. Today, he would marry the woman he loved.

"George, when Rose awakes, take her to my parents' house. I'll be there as soon as possible," he said.

"Yes, sir."

"Oh and take my suit," he told the man. "It's lying on the bed. Along with my suitcases."

As he trotted the horse out of the stables, the servants opened the gate and he spurred his mare down the street.

What a beautiful morning. The sun was shining brightly, and he knew later today, they would be outside in his parents' garden celebrating their love. Very few people were out and about on the street this early in the morning.

As he rounded the corner onto the main street, five men

jumped out in front of him and he pulled on the reins causing his horse to rear.

"What the hell?"

A man pointed a gun at him. "Get off your horse, now."

Hayden sighed. They were going to kill him on his wedding day.

"Now or the horse is dead," he said loudly.

Slowly, he slid from his mount, not wanting them to harm the animal.

"You were in a hurry. You got someplace to go?" the man said with an evil grin.

They knew. Someone had alerted them that they were going to be married today.

A man came up from behind him and shoved a potato sack over his head. He struggled, knowing that if he didn't fight them now, he probably never would have the chance.

Suddenly, an explosion of pain filled his head and he felt himself slumping to the ground. His last thoughts were of Rose.

CHAPTER 27

*R*ose stood dressed in her wedding gown looking down at the garden at the people gathered there. His mother had set up an archway and filled it with flowers. There were candles lit and the justice of the peace stood waiting for the ceremony to begin.

Sadie stood beside her gazing at the people. The ceremony was supposed to have started thirty minutes ago.

Rose paced the floor. "What's the problem. Why haven't they told me to come down?"

Sadie chewed her lip. "I don't know. Let me go see if I can find out."

As she stared out the window, she gazed at the spot where Hayden should be waiting for her. He wasn't there. His sisters were all sitting in chairs, waiting, and a few close family friends, but his mother and father and Hayden were missing.

Could his father be causing them problems? What if he refused to let Hayden marry her? But then her soon-to-be husband was old enough to marry her without his father's permission. What if he'd changed his mind?

Suddenly the door opened and Hayden's mother walked through. Rose could see the worry etched on her beautiful face. Something was wrong. Very wrong.

"Oh, you look so beautiful," she cried. "That dress looks gorgeous on you."

Her compliments were sweet, but Rose could see the concern on her face and it frightened her.

"Why hasn't the ceremony started? Where is Hayden? Is he here?"

His mother sighed and gripped her hands together. "Hayden has not shown up. I've sent a servant over to the house to see if there was a delay. Did you see him at all this morning?"

Fear clutched Rose's heart. "No. He had already left before I woke up. Last night, he insisted that we not see each other until the ceremony. Where could he have gone?"

All her fears suddenly rose and gripped her throat. Had he changed his mind? But he told her he loved her last night, but because she didn't respond with the words, could he have decided this marriage would never work for him?

"We talked into the wee hours of the night, sitting on the floor with his bedroom door between us. Do you think he changed his mind?"

His mother and Sadie moved to her and wrapped their arms around her. "I don't think so. My son is so in love with you. I can see it in his eyes. My biggest fear is that something has happened to him."

Suddenly Sadie stiffened. "Nellie. That damn Nellie Robinson. She would do this to stop your marriage. She's a gold digger and she wants a rich husband. Any rich man."

Rose walked out of their arms and sank on the bed, her legs almost giving out from her. "Maybe. But why wouldn't she have told my father and they would have come after me. They wouldn't harm Hayden, would they? They're Christian men. My father is a pastor. I can understand them coming after me, but not Hayden."

The two women sat on the bed beside her and each picked up a hand.

"I had planned to sing a song to Hayden today at our ceremony. One that proclaimed my love for him. I haven't had the chance to tell him I love him and I was going to do that today, but now I may never have that chance if someone has taken him. I'm so scared."

His mother stood. "We have to find him. At first, I just thought he was late, but I don't believe for a second that he would have backed out of marrying you. Something is wrong and I'm going to get my husband. The men need to go talk to Nellie. Find out what she's done, and if my son dies because of this witch, I'll make certain no man in town wants her. Ever."

Tears began to flow down Rose's cheeks. "Oh dear God, he can't be dead because of me. Please, nothing can happen to him."

"I'll be right back, Rose," Sadie said, "I'm going to go speak to Levi. If anyone can get to Nellie, it's him."

The two women ran out of the room and Rose felt like her heart broke. Great hulking sobs rose from her chest and she cried like she had not cried in years.

Hayden, her Hayden was missing. And it was all her fault. When she finally realized that she loved him, something happened to him. And it was all her fault.

Suddenly there was a knock on the door. She didn't look up, because she didn't care unless it was Hayden. She knew he would never see her before the ceremony.

"Rose," a familiar voice said. "It's time you came home."
Her head jerked up to gaze into her mother's eyes.
"If you want Hayden to live, you'll come back with me."

CHAPTER 28

Sadie hurried down the stairs, lifting her dress and all but running. When she reached the garden area, she glanced around and didn't see Levi. Tessa frowned at her and she motioned for her to come with her.

"Have you seen Levi?"

"No," Tessa said frowning. "What's going on? Everyone is sitting and wondering if this wedding is going to happen."

As they walked toward the street, Sadie said, "Hayden is missing. He left the house this morning and hasn't arrive here."

Tessa's mouth widened with surprise and yet she kept her stride up with Sadie's fast one. "Did he back out?"

"We don't know, but Nellie learned about the wedding and I'm afraid she's done something."

They reached the street and Sadie stepped out and hailed a cab. She gave the man the address where Nellie lived. Climbing in, the two women talked. Sadie had no idea what she would do once they reached Nellie's home, but by God, they would do something to make that bitch talk.

"What do you think has happened?" Tessa asked.

"I'm afraid that Nellie told Rose's father and somehow he has taken Hayden. By capturing Hayden, the wedding won't happen and he could possibly lure Rose back to him."

Tessa sighed and shook her head. "That old man is a conniving son of a bitch."

"Did you bring your pistol?"

The carriage was rough as it bounced along the streets. Sadie had to hang on, and she wished that Levi was there with her.

"Always," she said quietly. "Who are we going to kill? Nellie?"

Sadie laughed. "Don't tempt me. But if we try to rescue Hayden, then I thought we might need some firepower."

"Why didn't you bring Levi?"

"I couldn't find him. I looked all over the house before I came outside. If anyone can get to Nellie, it's him. But I don't know where he is."

They rode through the residential area where Nellie lived. When they pulled up to the house, Levi was dismounting his horse. Thank God, he was here.

"Don't leave," Sadie told the driver. "We will probably need to go somewhere else."

"Yes, ma'am," he said with a worried look.

The two women ascended from the carriage and walked up the drive just as Nellie answered Levi's knock on the door.

"Well, what do I owe the pleasure," she said, batting her eyes at Levi.

Sadie was ready to smack her right there.

Her eyes widened when she saw Sadie and Tessa step up beside Levi.

"Sadie," Levi said.

"What did you do, Nellie?" Sadie asked. "Did you go to Rose's father?"

"Of course not," she said with a lying smile. Sadie knew what she'd done.

Levi took Sadie's hand and squeezed it. "Nellie, Hayden is missing. Rose is waiting for him at his home. If they kill him, you could be implicated for murder."

Her eyes widened and she licked her lips nervously.

"Rose's father might be using him for bait to draw his daughter back into the fold," Levi said. "If they kill him, you will be going to jail."

"He's a reverend. He's not going to kill Hayden, you're just trying to frighten me."

Levi shook his head. "You don't understand the gravity of this situation. Her father will do anything to keep them apart, including killing Hayden. One less sinner in the world. And you will have led to Hayden's death."

Nellie swallowed nervously and it was all Sadie could do not to reach out and punch her.

Tessa opened her reticle and pulled out her pistol and casually checked the bullets and spun the barrel. "Yep, it's loaded and ready." Casually, she acted like she was going to point it at Nellie.

The girl's eyes widened. "All right, I went to the church and told her mother and father."

"Did they say anything?"

"All they said was thank you. It was really disappointing. I thought they would be happy, but they didn't say anything other than *Thank you* and *God Bless* me when I left. I don't understand those people."

Of course, she didn't and most spiritual people were

wonderful, but this sect of worshippers were strange and a little too strict for Sadie's way of thinking.

"They didn't tell you anything about their plans or if they were going to kidnap Hayden?"

"No," she said with a start. "Wait, they did mention a revival at Inspiration Point."

They all looked at each other. Levi nodded. "There are steep cliffs in that section of the city in just that area."

"We've got to go," Sadie said.

"I'll follow behind you," Levi replied.

"But, wait, I want to go," Nellie cried.

"No," all three of them said at the same time.

Unable to stop herself, Sadie doubled up her fist and then she punched Nellie. She felt her skin break where she hit the woman. "And that's for being such a bitch and telling Rose's father. If Hayden dies, I will tell the sheriff what you did."

They turned and walked away from the woman, shaking their heads.

"She's never going to learn," Tessa said. "Someday someone is going to put a bullet through her."

"No," Sadie said. "She's too mean to die."

CHAPTER 29

*R*ose glared at her mother. "What have you done with him?"

"Your father is holding him until you come home," she said. "I have a carriage waiting outside for you."

Stunned, she stared at her mother. "How did you get in here?"

The woman who had birthed her smiled. Why were they doing this to Rose? All her life, she'd felt different from them, like they weren't really her parents and she wasn't really their child.

She didn't belong with them.

"I walked in like I was supposed to be here," she said. "After all, I am the mother of the bride."

"Everyone here knows that you don't want me to marry Hayden."

Why did this feel like her parents had won? That she had to return home in order to save the man she loved.

"No one stopped me," she said smiling. "Sometimes when

you dress plain and keep your head down, people don't notice you."

All her life, she had been preached at that a woman was to appear plain and her mother followed her father's teachings. Anyone who dressed in bright colors was a Jezebel.

"Don't you want something better for me?" she asked her. "Don't you want me to be happy?"

Her mother shook her head. "Such a stubborn girl. You know our beliefs. Our teachings. Happiness is not something we shall experience until we get to heaven. You would do well to learn that lesson, now."

Sadness overwhelmed Rose. They had the man she loved and now she feared they would never be allowed to marry.

"The dress is lovely, but not appropriate. I brought you clothes to wear."

Tears welled in Rose's eyes. On what was supposed to be her happiest day, she felt nothing but sadness. Even the wedding gown she'd chosen they would take away from her.

She would be humiliated and made to repent her sins in front of the congregation. But if it would save Hayden, then she would do it.

"I'm not going unless you promise me that Hayden will be released once I return."

A sigh escaped her mother. "You know I have no power to promise that. It's your father's decision. But if you return with me, then his chances of being released are much higher. If you don't, all I can say is an eye for an eye."

The words sent chills down Rose's spine. She had no choice. If she wanted Hayden to live, then she would have to sacrifice herself.

"If the reverend harms him in any way, you better be

prepared for me to become even more rebellious. If he lets him go, I will marry Pastor Moore."

Her mother smiled. "You know I'm powerless."

Like all the women in the church were weak and incapable.

"And that's why I can't believe you would go along with this. That you don't want your daughter to be happy. I've fallen in love with Hayden, and even now, I could be carrying his child."

Her mother slapped her. Dumbfounded, she stepped back, shocked that she would resort to violence.

"So much wickedness resides in you. You will definitely need the cleansing ritual."

Astonished, she stared at her mother. Why was Rose so different from her family? Why did they seem like heretics?

Rose shuddered. Only once had she witnessed the cleansing ritual and she'd been horrified at what she'd seen. A poor woman tried to run away from her husband and had been caught. Afterward, the woman had been defeated. Never again had she tried to run away. Never again did she smile. Eventually the woman died.

But even that, Rose would endure if it saved Hayden's life.

"Get dressed, before someone comes in," her mother hissed. "You're going home today. You've done enough damage. Your father gave me one hour to bring you back before he began to torture the young man."

Rose wanted to resist. She wanted to scream but was fearful for Hayden. If this would save his life, then she would do what she must.

Her arms reached up to unbutton the back of the beautiful gown. Her mother came around to help her.

"You will no longer be living in our home. You will wed

Pastor Moore today. I'm surprised he's still willing to have you. Tonight, you will travel to his home in Abilene where you will be under lock and key until your husband can trust you."

They were not going to give her a chance to escape. All of the privileges she'd been allowed would be taken away until they were certain that her wicked spirit lived no more.

"Mother, I feel sorry for you. Have you never craved freedom? Never wanted to be a woman who could dress in bright colors. Never wanted to have friends?"

"I have friends," her mother said. "The women in the parish are my friends."

Her mother lived in a delusional world. Those women did nothing but criticize her.

"Those women talk bad about you all the time. You're never enough and they like nothing better than making the reverend's wife their target."

The dress slid to the floor and her mother gasped. "Take those indecent undergarments off right now."

What was wrong with her white satin pantaloons and shift? The corset held up her breasts and trimmed her waist.

She pulled out of her bag a pair of gray pantaloons and shift. Coarse material that Rose knew would rub her sensitive skin raw.

Sadness overwhelmed Rose as she put on her everyday plain garments once again. The only beautiful clothes she had ever worn were the ones Hayden's mother helped her purchase. Even the ballgowns she had worn were plain and gray. Nothing colorful.

When she was dressed, her mother gave her a bonnet to wear.

"Make certain your hair is up inside. It's not to be seen."

"Yes, ma'am," she automatically replied.

"Now, we're going to leave and go down through the servants' quarters. Do not give me any trouble, young lady. We have barely enough time to reach Inspiration Point."

They were going to Inspiration Point? There were steep cliffs there and a chill ran down her spine. Why were they going there?

"Why there?"

Her mother smiled. "Your father is holding a revival. A chance for sinners to repent and you are going to repent."

CHAPTER 30

*H*ayden awoke tied to a chair on the side of a makeshift stage, his head pounding. Behind him, the big tent provided shade, but where they had him sitting, the sun was baking him.

The cliffs of Inspiration Point showed the city of Fort Worth below. Normally, this was one of his favorite places.

Bright sunlight from the Texas sun had sweat pouring down his face. Someone splashed water on him and he realized they wanted him awake for some reason. Then he saw the man he knew he would always hate.

"Mr. Lee, bow your head and confess your sins," the reverend shouted at him.

What sins was he talking about? What had Hayden done wrong besides take care of the man's daughter. Keep her safe and love her. If that was a sin, then he wanted to be a sinner.

"Mr. Lee, I will give you one more chance to confess your sins before this crowd and ask for the Lord for his forgiveness."

Then he noticed a crowd of people sitting out front,

watching. About fifty people were gathered inside the makeshift tent out of the sun.

"What sins are you talking about?" he moaned, the sun making his head pound even worse.

"The sin of fornication and adultery. You took my innocent daughter from me," he shouted. "Did you sleep with her?"

There was no way he would ever admit to this man what he and Rose shared. It was none of his business and he would not publicly humiliate the woman he loved.

"We were to be married today," Hayden said. "But your men dragged me away." Louder he yelled, "You're holding me against my will. Release me now."

How could these people just sit and watch this? Didn't they see that this was wrong? Couldn't they tell he was in pain? No one in the crowd moved to help him.

"I will repeat. Did you sleep with my daughter? Ruin her good name?"

They could torture him all they wanted, but he was not going to harm Rose by admitting they spent one night in each other's arms. His focus had to remain on his love for Rose.

"I love your daughter. I want to marry her."

The crowd started to boo and he wasn't certain whose side they were on. They were not moving to help him.

The reverend glanced out at them and Hayden could see his uneasiness.

"Are you a man of God?"

"I was raised a Methodist," he said. "If this is a church, I don't know what kind it is. Most religious people don't hit people in the head and then tie them up."

"Silence," the reverend said.

The men who had captured him suddenly surrounded

him. They laid their hands on his shoulders and the reverend began to pray.

At first, Hayden wasn't worried, but then he focused on the words.

"Lord, Rose is my daughter and this man has defiled her with his lust. You say an eye for an eye, a tooth for a tooth. But what about a daughter? In the old testament they stoned the adulterers. Justice will be yours, but revenge will be mine."

What? The old man was mixing up scripture and making it to his own demands.

"Amen," the reverend said.

A group of women began to sing in the corner and then Hayden saw Rose. Her hands were tied together as they lead her toward the alter.

She gasped when she saw him, her eyes filling with tears.

"I'm sorry," she mouthed.

He tried to grin, but every muscle in his body ached, and he feared what these men surrounding him were about to do. Slowly, he began to work at the ropes on his wrist. If he wanted to live, he had to get untied. He had to reach Rose and help her.

They led Rose to the stage. When they reached the center, the choir stopped singing.

"My daughter, you are a wicked Jezebel. You must be punished. Your lover must be punished and then you will marry a fine young man of my choosing, John Moore. I'm your father. I decide who is to be your husband. In our faith, the women are subservient to their husbands. On your knees."

The women pushed her down.

"Has the cleansing ritual been done?"

"Yes, Reverend," her mother said. "Her sins were scrubbed from her body."

What the hell? Rose did not deserve this humiliation.

"You've disappointed me, my daughter. Your focus is on the world and not on the laws of God. I had chosen you a husband and now you will marry him."

Hayden screamed, "No."

One of the men standing next to him smacked him, almost knocking him out again. Pretending to be unconscious, Hayden let his head tip to the side, then the group of males surrounding him left to approach a man on the stage.

His fingers, again, began to work on the ties around his wrists. Suddenly he felt fingers at his wrist but didn't dare turn around. Who was helping him?

"Hurry," Hayden whispered.

"Daughter," the reverend commanded from on stage, "this is the godly man I have chosen for you. Now you will wed."

Hayden watched through barely open eyes as tears streamed down Rose's cheeks.

"I will never make you happy. Your life will be a living hell," she said with defiance.

Her father slapped her. "Silence."

Suddenly Hayden's wrists were free and he felt tugging at the ties on his feet.

It seemed to take forever and he feared that at any moment, the men would turn around and find him loose. The sham of a ceremony began.

"John, do you take this woman to be your wife, to—"

The rope pulling away from his ankles, he leaped to his feet and ran toward Rose.

He reached the reverend, whose eyes grew wide, and punched him, knocking him to the ground. John tried to grab him, and Rose punched him and gave him a kick.

Hayden grabbed Rose and they ran, but the men

surrounded them. Levi, Sadie, and even Tessa rushed to their sides.

"Let them go," Levi warned. "This fight is over."

Tessa pulled out her gun. The woman could send a tin can into next week, her aim was that good.

"Don't make me hurt you," she said, pointing her gun at the men.

Stupidly, they didn't believe or know about her skills. After all, she was just a woman. When a man reached for Rose, she put a bullet in his arm. The man screamed, falling back.

"The next one will be in your heart," she warned. "And I can reload almost as fast as I can fire. As mad as I am right now, don't tempt me or all of you will meet your maker today."

Hayden squeezed Rose's arm and she gave a little whimper. "Come on, let's get out of here."

They were trying to get out of the tent, but the crowd was before them and her father's men behind them.

Outside the covering, a carriage rolled up. A shout from the back came and he realized it was his mother, father, and the sheriff.

"What the hell is going on here?" the sheriff said, strolling into the tent.

The reverend gave him an evil smile and walked toward the man. "So good to see you, Sheriff. This man is trying to steal my daughter again."

The sheriff laid his hand on his gun and leaned back, gazing at the reverend.

"Now, Reverend, you wouldn't be lying would you? Seems to me these two kids were trying to get married today. Did you take Hayden against his will?"

Her father's face turned red. "She's my daughter. She's been missing. And he's had her the entire time."

Rose turned on her father. "No, you forced me to live with him because I was staying with Sadie until you surrounded her home. Hayden has been an innocent in all of this. Sheriff, I want you to know I am never going back to my parents' home. These men were trying to stop us from leaving. I'm going and if you dare interfere with my life again, I will file charges. Do you understand?"

Then she turned to her mother. "And you, dear Mother, need to experience the cleansing ritual."

Rose lifted her sleeve and there was a gasp. "Never come near me again."

Hayden was stunned. Her skin was raw. Carefully, he took her hand and they walked toward his parents and their carriage. His friends surrounded them, just daring someone to try to stop them from leaving.

A thought occurred. He remembered his horse. "Sheriff, they took my horse. I think it's called horse stealing. Arrest them."

The men's eyes grew wide and they began to stutter.

"You have one hour to get my horse back to my house," he told them. "One hour or I'm filing charges. Horse stealing is a hanging offense here in Texas. Your choice. Live or die."

When they reached the carriage, Rose gingerly hugged Sadie, then Tessa, and even Levi. "Thank you for coming. Thank you for being our friends and rescuing us."

Hayden felt his heart almost break in two. They were both hurting, but he could see the pain in her eyes and it was more than just physical.

"I'm just sorry we didn't get here sooner," Tessa said.

"Go home and rest. We'll talk soon," Sadie said.

Hayden clasped Levi. "Thanks, man. I couldn't have done it without you."

"Go take care of your woman," Levi told him. "Whatever they did to her, she's in pain."

The reverend was arguing with the sheriff. The man was refusing to accept defeat and the sheriff was just standing there watching the craziness spill out of him.

Suddenly there was a shout and Hayden whirled round in time to see Pastor Moore point his gun at Hayden.

Immediately, Hayden fell on top of Rose. She screamed and he knew he had hurt her, but he'd been trying to protect her.

The sheriff grabbed Pastor Moore's arm and pulled it towards him. The gun went off, the bullet striking the Reverend.

"Pastor Moore shot the reverend," Levi shouted.

People rushed to the edge of the cliffs, where the force of the bullet had sent the Reverend over the edge, to see if he was still alive.

The sheriff knocked the gun from John's hand, whirled him around and handcuffed him.

As Hayden rose off of Rose, she groaned.

"Do you want to check on him?"

"No, I want you to take me home," she said and curled up next to him on the carriage bench.

His father reached out and lifted her sleeve.

With a sound of disgust, he shook his head. "No, we're taking you to a doctor. Does the rest of your skin look like that?"

A tear trickled down her cheek.

"Yes," she said.

Taking her hand, his father stared at her. "Rose, I didn't

want you to marry my son, because I didn't want him to leave Fort Worth. But, somehow, we'll make this work. Welcome to the family. You're our daughter."

Hayden smiled at his father and his mother. "Can we wait a few days for Rose to heal and then marry?"

His mother reached out and took her other hand. "Of course. Once Rose is feeling better, we'll get you two wedded."

Hayden pulled Rose as close as he dared. "No one will ever harm you again," he promised. "Never."

The carriage pulled away and Rose glanced back at her father's congregation. She never wanted to see any of them again.

CHAPTER 31

*H*ayden opened the door to Rose's room and peeked in. His heart wrenched in his chest at the burns on her skin. The doctor said she would completely heal, but he had let her down.

No one should've had to endure the way the women in her father's church had used a wire brush to rid her of her sins. And if he ever learned their names, they would suffer the same type of punishment.

Watching her sleep, he wondered if she still wanted to marry him. After all, he had not been able to keep her safe. And because of his weakness, she was now hurting.

She looked so beautiful sleeping in bed, but he knew she suffered. The doctor had advised her to wear very little clothing to let her skin heal. Looking her over, the man had been angry, furious, that someone would do this to another human being.

Which only made Hayden's guilt even worse. The poor woman had agreed to return to her father's church to save him.

Who knows what they would have done to him given half the chance? But for her to endure this kind of humiliation for him, left him hurting.

If her father wasn't already dead and her mother hadn't left town, he would go after both of them. No parent should ever inflict this kind of pain on their daughter.

How did they go from here?

Suddenly, her eyes opened and she stared at him. "Hayden? Are you all right?"

What could he say? That the pain of her suffering was eating him alive. When all he wanted to do was go out and put a bullet in the people who had harmed her?

"I'm fine. Just checking on you," he said with a lie.

He wasn't fine.

She patted to the bed. "Come, sit beside me."

Eagerly he entered the bedroom and sat beside her, wanting to lie down beside her and pull her into his arms. The need to hold her was strong, but he knew that would only cause her more pain.

"How are you feeling?"

"Better, but my skin aches," she said, gazing at him.

He tried to hide his emotions, but somehow they must have shown.

"I will heal," she said softly. "Just give me some time. Did you speak to the sheriff?"

"Yes," he said, not wanting her to know that there was really nothing the sheriff could do since this was a common practice in their religion.

"He's not going to do anything is he?"

"No," he said, wanting to rush out the door and go after the women who had done this to her.

"I've been told that we both have to put this behind us," he said, almost gritting his teeth. "I'm sorry, Rose."

She reached out and patted his arm. "It's not your fault. I should have been more prepared for her to sneak in. I'm just so thankful that you were not more seriously harmed."

The only real harm he'd suffered was to his pride. His ability to take care of Rose and it made him doubt everything. As much as he loved her, could he keep her safe?

"We were lucky," he said quietly.

"Are you all right?" she asked her dark brown eyes gazing at him filled with concern.

"I'm fine," he said, not willing to share with her how guilty he felt at letting her be injured while under his care.

Never again would anyone sneak in and harm them. There was extra protection around his home and if and when they married, those same men would protect Rose at his parent's home. They would travel with them to New York.

Did she still want to marry him? He had doubts because of his lack of taking care of her. But what about Rose?

"Do you still want to marry me?"

Her head jerked around and she stared at him. "Yes, but are you certain you want to marry me?"

"I love you, Rose," he said softly. "Yes, I want to marry you."

"Then what's wrong?"

He started to tell her but then he realized he would be admitting to a weakness and no man wanted his wife to think of him as weak.

"Nothing is wrong. As soon as you're feeling better, we'll marry," he said. "Until then, you should rest."

She gazed at him with her eyes shining with unshed tears.

"If you've changed your mind, it's all right," she said softly.

"I can understand how no one would want to put up with my crazy family."

He hadn't had the guts to tell her, her father was dead. Not yet. Not while she was so ill. When she was better, then he would tell her, but not now. And her mother had disappeared. Not even checking on Rose to see how she was feeling before she left.

No, he was her family now.

"It's been a rough couple of days. I just want you to get better and then we'll marry," he said, squeezing her hand. "Now rest."

Leaning down, he kissed her on the forehead, wishing he could kiss her and show her his feelings, but knowing right now she needed to rest.

Standing, he walked to the door. "I'll have the cook bring you up something to eat."

She nodded and then rolled her head toward the wall.

They just needed time to heal from what her father had done. Time to get over the pain and then they could begin their life together.

he doctor gave her two tins of a salve to put on the brush marks that marred her skin. The first day she had slept for hours, her body and soul healing from the trauma.

Poor Hayden checked on her every few hours, though the doctor had ordered him to bed as well. He had a nasty bump on his head where they knocked him out.

His horse had been returned later that day and he had not pressed charges. The congregation had been warned to stay away from Rose or charges of harming someone would be filed against all of them.

So far, no one had come near the house.

Now a week later, she was starting to feel like her old self.

"Miss Tuttle, you have visitors. Should I show them in?" Melody asked.

"Who is it?" she asked, not wanting to see just anyone.

"Your friends, Sadie and Tessa," the maid said. The staff had been overly protective of her and had catered to her every need. Already, she loved them for taking care of her.

A smile spread across her face. "Yes, please let them in."

The doctor had told her to try to keep material from her skin. Between the salve and being almost naked most of the time, she'd stayed in her room.

Hayden had visited her, but there was a tenseness between them that she hadn't expected.

Sadie was the first through the door. In her hand, she held a bouquet of flowers. She reached for her hand. "I'm so happy to see you. How are you feeling?"

Her friends would see the depression. They would know she was sad, and yet, she tried to hide it from them.

"I'm better. Not as sore as I was. In a few days, I should be back to normal."

"Oh hell, that means she'll make us to take her to the saloon and let her sing," Tessa said, walking in the door.

They sat on the edge of her bed. "Are you doing all right?"

Tears welled in her eyes. "No. Hayden won't answer my questions about my father. What happened after we left?"

Tessa and Sadie took her hands. "Your father was killed when he fell over the cliff. The sheriff said his head hit a rock. Your mother went into shock and…"

"And what?" Rose pushed, hearing the anxiety in her friend's voice.

Tessa shook her head. "She packed up the kids and left town."

Sadness overwhelmed Rose. How could a mother subject her daughter to being cleansed of her sins with a wire brush? It hurt just thinking of the humiliation she'd suffered as the women scrubbed her sins from her naked body.

Sighing, Rose worried about her brother and sister. Would they be subjugated to the same type of abuse? But now, they were gone. Someday she would find them. No child should suffer the way they all had.

"What did they use on you, Rose?" Tessa asked. "I'd like to take it and let those women experience what you did."

Rose loved her friends. They were always on her side. "A wire brush. They had to make certain that my sins were removed."

Sadie growled. "Dear God. We were trying to find you. Oh, Nellie went to your father. Maybe she's the one who needs her sins scrubbed from her body."

"I'm not surprised," Rose told her. "Did you see Mrs. Griffin's article in the paper?" The woman had written a recent article declaring that Rose received what she deserved.

Laughter exploded from Sadie. "Yes, I read it and Levi kicked her out of the hotel and now he's trying to get her fired from the newspaper. Oh, and someone named George delivered a whole wheelbarrow of horse manure to the newspaper office she works out of."

A smile crossed Rose's face. The article had been about how Nellie had tried to save Hayden from a bad girl.

"I never told him to," Rose said with a grin. "I've been in bed for the last week."

"Look, I can't imagine what you've been through and I know you've been in pain," Sadie said. "We've been so worried about you, but Hayden wouldn't let us see you. He said you needed to rest. Then today, he spoke to Levi and told us he thought you needed us."

"He did?" she asked, thinking her husband-to-be must have noticed her sadness. "I'm worried about me and Hayden. He hasn't been his usual self."

He'd been withdrawn and not the loving man she adored. They couldn't let this come between them.

"Honey, he's been worried sick about you," Sadie said. "He even spoke to the doctor about how he's so afraid you were getting infected."

Tessa shook her head. "Give the man a break. He was captured. Men like to protect their women and he probably feels like he failed. And to almost have to watch you marry another man, that must have terrified him."

"He's crazy in love with you," Sadie said.

Tears flowed down her cheeks. "When I realized he was missing, I was so afraid. I realized then how much I loved him. If something had happened to him because of me, I couldn't have lived with myself."

They had come so close to losing one another. Now, she just wanted things to return to normal.

"Give yourself some time," Tessa said. "Soon, the two of you will be back to your usual selves, but right now, you've suffered a huge trauma."

Rose nodded.

"And no matter what happens, we always love our parents. So you're grieving for the loss of your father."

She stared at Sadie. What an unusual thing to say, but maybe it was true. Her father had not been all bad, but in the last few years, he'd grown more strict with his religious demands. Maybe she was grieving for the parent she had loved.

"You know, I miss my father, but the *Reverend*, I will never miss. In my mind, they are two different people. The Reverend was so consumed with his idea of religion and my father was the man who loved me."

They were silent for a moment.

"Have you and Levi decided on a date yet?"

"I was just about to ask you the same question," Sadie said.

"Next Saturday. The doctor said I would be healed by then. Right now, I can't stand for anyone to touch anywhere but my hands."

Sadie smiled. "We've decided on a November wedding. Right before Thanksgiving."

"What about you, Tessa?"

"Oh, I'm not getting married. But I do think I'm going to enter that rifle competition as a man. I've got me some britches and I'm going to be their worst nightmare."

They all laughed.

"You've got too many curves to be considered a man," Rose said.

She grinned. "Thank you, but I think I can bind my breasts. Pile my hair up, put on enough black makeup to make me look like I have a scruffy beard and win the competition."

"I have complete faith in your ability. You're going to bring home the national competition grand prize."

Rose stared at her friends. Where would she be without them? With a sigh, she grasped their hands. "No matter what happens, I'm so glad you two are always by my side."

"And we always will be," Sadie said.

"You know, you're going off to New York and you're going to become a big star. You may not want to be around us any longer," Tessa said.

Laughter bubbled up from Rose. "As much as I love to sing and that's always been my dream, right now, I just want to marry Hayden."

"And you will," Tessa said.

"Yes," Sadie agreed. "Soon."

CHAPTER 33

*H*ayden was nervous. Once again, it was their wedding day, and this time, he had the ring. Rose had spent the night at his parents and he'd stayed home alone. The last two weeks had been stressful.

Once, he almost called off the wedding, not because he didn't love her, but because he'd failed her.

Because of him, she'd suffered a great harm and it was hard to forgive himself for letting her be hurt. Levi told him no man could have protected her from her crazy father and he had to believe that was true.

But never again would he ever allow anyone to hurt Rose. He didn't care who they thought they were.

The sun was shining brightly. He glanced out the window down into the garden and smiled at his sisters laughing and giggling and being their usual mischievous selves. He was a lucky man who had a family that loved him.

A knock sounded on the door and his father entered.

He gazed at him and smiled. "Big day."

"Yes," Hayden said, glancing back to the garden.

"Your mother wanted me to have a talk with you," he said.

Hayden turned and smiled at him. "About the wedding night? I think I've got that all taken care of."

Laughter came from his father. "I didn't want to tell her that. But I said I would speak to you."

"Good, you can tell her we spoke about what is going to happen."

His father smiled. "There is one thing I want to say to you." He paused. "Since the day you rescued Rose, you've not been yourself. Son, don't blame yourself for what happened. We didn't know they were going to capture you. Her own mother somehow sneaked into our house and took Rose away. Which just galls me to no end. The very idea of that woman walking up here without anyone stopping her is frightening."

Hayden understood his father's feelings. There were six young women living under his roof and that proved how easily someone could snatch them away.

"What I'm trying to say is this wasn't your fault. Rose getting hurt was terrible, but if anyone is to blame, it's her mother who I've heard has disappeared."

"Yes, the sheriff told me. He would have issued charges against her if she had not left in the middle of the night."

What kind of church believed you could scrub your sins away? What kind of mother did that to her daughter?

"It feels like I didn't protect her like I should have," he admitted, knowing it would hurt to say those words.

"Son, you've done so much for her. I can see in your eyes that you love her very much and you would never intentionally let someone harm her. Put this behind you. Enjoy today. Yes, I wish you weren't going to New York, but you are and it's my fervent wish that you'll return here someday."

Hayden gave his father a hug. "Thanks, Papa. You and

Mother have shown me what I want in a marriage and I just hope I can give that to Rose."

"And I, son, hope she will love you the way your mother loves me."

Levi burst into the room grinning at the two of them. "The preacher is waiting on us."

"It's time," Hayden said, suddenly feeling lighter. His bride was waiting for him to show up in the garden, and this time, he would not disappoint her. This time, their wedding was going to happen.

Ten minutes later, he watched as his bride walked toward him. His father was her escort and that made him proud. The dress she'd chosen was beautiful and he knew he was the luckiest man alive.

When she reached him, she handed her bouquet to Sadie and took his hands in hers. Then she began to sing to him. The song spoke of love and the notes wrapped around his heart and he realized what she was saying. She was telling him she loved him.

Tears welled in his eyes, and at the end, he pulled her into his arms and kissed her.

"I love you, Hayden. The moment I realized you had been kidnapped, my heart broke and I understood I'd fallen in love with you. That you were the most important person or *thing* in my life. Without you, my life would have no meaning. I'm so happy to be your wife."

They clung to one another, their foreheads resting against each other's.

"Rose, I've loved and waited so long to hear those words. This makes today even more special."

She laid her hand on his cheek and kissed him again.

The justice of the peace stood there staring at them. "I always thought the kissing came at the end of the ceremony," he finally said. "Should we begin?"

They broke apart, smiled at each other, and turned to face him.

"Let's get married," Rose said.

"Yes," Hayden replied. "We have a train to catch. To New York."

She grinned at him. "But my husband will always come first."

* * *

THANKS FOR READING RAVENOUS ROSE. I loved the idea of a songstress who when she sang, a man was enthralled with her and her voice. My hero Hayden, wanted her, but without the hassles of saying I do. Next up is Tempting Tessa. She's a little spitfire and so far I'm really loving how this book is turning out. For a sneak peek continue reading.

* * *

TESSA HARRIS KNEW she could win this competition. But men didn't like it when a woman beat them and they had done everything they could to keep her from entering the National Marksman Competition.

But she refused to be denied.

Dressed like a man, so far, no one questioned her identity. All her blonde hair was piled in a bun beneath her hat. She wore one of her father's western-cut shirts and a pair of pants that were baggy and loose to hide her well-defined hips. She had a fake mustache glued beneath her nose, and she'd tried to make her skin look unshaven. When she walked, she strode with a manly swagger.

Standing inside the arena in Fort Worth, Texas, she tried not to look directly at the people sitting on the benches, fearing her eyes giving her away. For one thing, her father sat there with her mother and two brothers. She feared her disguise would not fool them. And she worried her father would recognize her guns and his shirt.

Now they were down to the last two events with her and Seth Robinson knocking out the rest of the competition. She couldn't decide if she was going to remove her hat and let her curls down or simply walk away with the cash.

Most likely, she would walk away with the money and the chance to compete nationally.

Of all people, Seth Robinson, the mayor's son, a man she found incredibly handsome, who even caused a few flutters in her blood, was the man she would take down. Her eyes soaked in his broad shoulders, dark hair, high cheekbones, and a slight mustache over a full mouth with incredibly white teeth. When he smiled, those gorgeous lips of his generated tingles skipping down her spine.

An excellent marksman, but she was better. His good looks might serve him well with the ladies, but she was here to win.

Raised by a father who owned a gun smithery, she knew her guns to perfection. She could drill a bullet in a porcupine's butt from fifteen hundred yards with a rifle and make a tin can dance a jig with a six-shooter from fifty feet.

Tessa was the best and everyone in town knew it. And that's why she, aka Elton McClellan, had entered the competition. "Elton" would soon win the day.

"Good luck," Seth said to her, frowning when he glanced at her. Was her mustache on straight?

She reached up and patted it to make certain it remained in place.

Seth had a sister who Tessa had, on more than one occasion, considered using for target practice. Nellie Robinson stirred up more shit in this town than the cowboys down in Hell's Half Acre on a Saturday night.

The woman had almost cost both of her friends their happiness and someday someone was going to get tired of Nellie interfering. And that person could be Tessa.

With a nod, she replied in a deep, gravelly voice that sounded like she was in puberty. "You too."

"The winner buys the loser a beer when this is over," he said with a smile the ladies in town swooned over.

Oh, she would definitely be the winner. But there was no way she would fraternize with the enemy. And Seth was the enemy.

"I don't drink beer," she replied.

"Too bad, I thought maybe we could do some celebrating and maybe even find us a woman. There's a real pretty gal by the name of Tessa Harris who's probably a finer markswoman than either of us. We could look her up and have a private competition. Winner takes the woman."

With a quick swallow, she bit back the gasp that filled her throat. Like hell, winner takes the woman. Not without putting a bullet in them first.

"I'm not disrespectful toward women," she said and turned her back on him, focusing on the competition.

All she had to do was beat him and that would be completely satisfying. They would compete with both a rifle and a pistol. First, Tessa and then Seth.

While lying on the ground aiming her rifle, the wind suddenly picked up and she almost lost her hat. She waited until the breeze settled and then she aimed and fired at the target. All three shots knocked out the bull's-eye.

Standing, she moved to the next station, and in rapid succession, filled the center of the target, clearly leaving no room for error on Seth's part.

Walking away, she passed him. "Winner takes all."

A frown spread across his face.

Smiling, she moved away from the center of the arena to watch him aim and fire. With the rifle, it was too close to call, and when it came down to the six-shooter, he left a hole in the center of the bull's-eye.

The cash and the chance to compete were hers.

The crowd roared and the judge called them both to the podium in the center of the field. There, Nellie Robinson was waiting to award the prize. Five hundred dollars and a big ribbon showing first place.

With a smile on her face, Tessa hurried to the stage. When she got there, she and Seth stood off to the side as the judge went on and on about a great day of competition.

"Congratulations," Seth said. "That's some mighty fine shooting."

"Thank you," she said, remembering to make her voice sound manly.

"Where did you learn to shoot like that? I don't remember seeing you around here," Seth whispered.

"Haven't been here long," she said and realized that her voice didn't sound hoarse.

A frown appeared between his brows and she turned her back to him. Thank God, this would soon be over.

The hot Texas sun beat down on them and she just wished

they would hurry and hand her the prize money. She was ready to pocket that cash and celebrate.

Tessa would be traveling to Washington, D.C. to compete in the national championships.

Finally, Nellie came to stand in front of her with the check and the ribbon. It was all Tessa could do to keep from shouting at her, but she was doing her best to remain calm. No one needed to know who really won this competition.

"Congratulations," Nellie said, handing her the check then reached beneath her hat and hit the brim, knocking it to the ground, Tessa's blonde curls spilled down her shoulders.

A gasp came from the crowd as they all stared at her.

Nellie grinned and took back the check. "Your mustache is coming off. I knew it was you. And now you're disqualified. My brother wins."

Ugly laughter came from the woman that Tessa despised. Her friend, Sadie once socked Nellie, and Tessa resisted doing the same. It would only secure her spot in Mrs. Griffin's column in the newspaper.

The judge stood with his mouth open, staring at her. "Tessa Harris?"

"It's me, Judge."

"What a disgrace. You're disqualified."

Grabbing her hat, she turned to Seth. "You may have won the competition, but we'll always know who's the best. Enjoy my money."

"Winner takes all," he said with a grin.

Walking away, she wanted to slap him. She hated how her words had come back to bite her.

Now, not only had she lost the regional competition, she could never compete in the national competition. Now her father would be furious for her risking his business. Now she would be the talk of the gossips.

Once again, Tessa's actions made her a member of the Bad Girls' Club. And she proudly proclaimed her membership. Who wanted to be a good girl when all it got you was trouble?

To Continue Reading Go to Amazon!

\

PLEASE LEAVE A REVIEW

Did you enjoy the book? Reviews help authors. I would appreciate you posting a review.

Follow Sylvia McDaniel on Facebook.

Sign up for my new book alert http://www. sylviamcdaniel.com/sign-up-for-my-newsletter/ and receive a complimentary book.

DEADLY

LIPSTICK AND LEAD

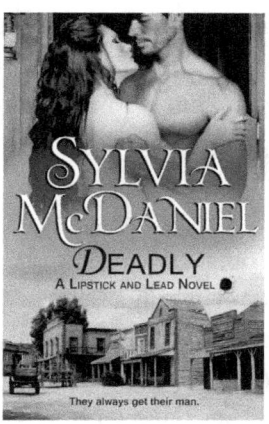

Meg McKenzie stood in yet another hotel room, another dusty frontier town, on the hunt for yet another wayward criminal. She pulled out her Baby Dragoon revolver from her holster, spun the cylinder, and checked to make sure a bullet graced every chamber. With a gentle tug, she checked the leather case, and then she slid the weapon back into its holster, just a fingertip away.

She wore her gun low on her hips just below the waist of her father's hand-me-down pants. No fancy dress for Meg.

"The McKenzie sisters are about to strike again," her sister Ruby said, as she slid her own gun into the hidden sheath-like case neatly tucked beneath her petticoats. Her saloon dress dipped low in the front, to the edge of her breasts, the straps completely off her shoulder. She flipped her blonde hair back and checked her image one last time in the mirror. "How many men have we brought to justice?"

In the last year, they had learned the bounty hunter trade and continued the legacy of their father. With his death, the girls had been forced to find work in order to save the farm and in a desperate moment chosen their current path. Meg and Ruby chased wanted criminals, and Annabelle maintained their family farm. At least until they returned and could join their sister once again. They'd never intended to make this their lifelong occupation. Just long enough to pay off the mortgage on the farm.

"At least twelve. Seems we've spent more time on the road than we have at home," Meg said, homesickness surging through her like an open wound.

"Just as well with Sheriff Zach still coming out to the house looking for you."

"Zach Gillespie wants a quiet, retiring woman who wears a dress and has tea parties. Do I look like that kind of woman?" Meg shook her head. Her heartache was nearly healed, though she could never look at Zach again without smiling and remembering him naked.

Ruby laughed. "No, but you could if you wanted."

Meg glanced out the window. The glow of the setting sun cast a shadow, but she could still see the dress shop down the street. After she'd spoken to this no-name town's sheriff, she'd spent time in the little dress shop, gazing and fingering the available dresses and the patterns of the latest fashions. Inside these pants, a woman longed to emerge and live like a lady, not the rough bounty hunter façade of a life she lived now.

"I'll never change for any man. As soon as we pay off the farm, then I'm going to begin my life and do things the way I want to," Meg vowed. She had dreams, she had plans, and soon, it would be her time.

Circumstances required she dress like a man. But the girly-girl in her had a hidden vice. Her own little secret pleasure...a rouge pot. Just a tiny bit of color to her lips helped her remember she was a girl. A girl who had the same desires as every other woman.

As the sun continued its descent, cloaking the street in darkness, she knew it would soon be time to carry out their plan.

"Your weapon's ready?" Meg asked one last time. She worried about Ruby and hated leaving her alone with the criminal they were chasing.

"Yes," Ruby said. "And you'll be there with me?"

"Until you give me the signal."

"Remind me how much this guy's worth?"

"Five hundred dollars." This could be their last bounty if things worked out like Meg planned.

Ruby smiled and walked over to the window. "Papa would be so proud of us."

Meg shook her head, knowing their Papa would have been furious at the chances they were taking. "Maybe secretly, but he'd tell us we should have taken jobs in town. He'd have been more concerned about our safety than how quickly we were paying off the farm."

Ruby turned, her mouth twisted with displeasure. "No. I

will never become a maid again. Never. This last year has been exciting, and criminals are too stupid to realize a pretty woman is going to pull a gun on them."

Meg nodded. In the last year, Ruby had changed and matured. She'd gone from a love-crazed girl to being driven to catch as many low-life criminals as they could. She enjoyed the chase, the thrill. "Annabelle said we need six hundred dollars more, and the farm will be mortgage free."

"Old man Bates will fall out of his chair when you pay off the note."

Meg smiled. "Annabelle said he wasn't too friendly when she took in the payment on the note this year. He had plans on repossessing the farm. Too bad."

"I miss Annabelle," Ruby said, with a wistful whine in her voice.

"Yeah, me too. But someone had to take care of the farm, and she's good at the bookkeeping."

Meg glanced out the window and watched as men entered the saloon, the doors swinging wide. Now was when her nerves had her stomach rolling, her heart racing, and fear choking her throat. What if something happened to Ruby? How could she live with herself?

"The drinking has begun," Meg said quietly, listening to the music spilling out into the street from the local saloon.

"And will soon end for Simon Trudeau," Ruby said laughing, her eyes shining with excitement.

There was no fear in her gaze, only excited anticipation. Only reckless adventure. And that worried Meg.

"The horses are saddled and ready to go. Give me your satchel, and I'll secure it on your horse. I can't go in with you, or they'll make the connection between us." Meg stared at her youngest sister, fear sitting like a pit in the bottom of her stomach. "You're all set? Your weapons are ready?"

Ruby shrugged. "My knife is in my boot. My gun is in my holster." She smiled. "And my charm is ready to ensnare this poor bastard."

Meg was always stunned at how much Ruby enjoyed the chase. They used her as the bait, and then Meg would pull a gun on some poor unlucky bastard, and Ruby would tie him up. Every time before a catch, her blue eyes would sparkle and shine with excitement. She loved being a bounty hunter. She loved catching criminals, and most of all she loved playing her many roles.

They'd done everything from the distraught woman, pregnant wife, and now a saloon girl. Wherever the unlawful resided, they'd lay a trap and ensnare the wanted.

"Where's your hat?" Ruby asked.

"Right here," Meg said and picked up her black cowboy hat and pulled it down tight.

But for Meg it was just a job. A means to an end. A way to earn a decent living and pay for the farm. Once they had enough money, she would retire and never chase another criminal. But Ruby loved the chase, the entrapment, and the thrill of turning in the longrider.

Music echoed down the street, and Meg knew it was time. "Are you ready?"

Ruby smiled, her lips painted red, her cheeks tinted with the same color. "Let's get this done, so we can go home for a while."

"Let's go."

The two walked out of the hotel room together, but once they reached the street, Ruby walked to the saloon alone.

Meg gave her just enough time to get inside, and then she followed. Time to go to work.

To Continue Reading Go To Amazon!

Also By Sylvia McDaniel
Western Historicals
A Hero's Heart
Second Chance Cowboy
Ethan

American Brides
**Katie: Bride of Virginia

Angel Creek Christmas Brides
**Charity
**Ginger
**Minne
**Cora

Bad Girls of the West
Scandalous Sadie
Ravenous Rose
Tempting Tessa
Nellie's Redemption

The Burnett Brides Series
The Rancher Takes A Bride
The Outlaw Takes A Bride
The Marshal Takes A Bride
The Christmas Bride
Boxed Set

Lipstick and Lead Series
Desperate
Deadly

Dangerous
Daring
**Determined
Deceived
Defiant
Devious
Lipstick and Lead Box Set Books 1-4
Lipstick and Lead Box Set Books 5-9
Lipstick and Lead Box Set Books 1-9
**Quinlan's Quest

Mail Order Bride Tales
**A Brother's Betrayal
**Pearl
**Ace's Bride

Scandalous Suffragettes of the West
**Abigail
Bella
Mistletoe Scandal

Southern Historical Romance
A Scarlet Bride

The Cuvier Women
Wronged
Betrayed
Beguiled
Boxed Set

The Debutante's of Durango
The Debutante's Scandal

The Debutante's Gamble
The Debutante's Revenge
The Debutante's Santa

** Denotes a sweet book.

**Want to learn about my new releases before anyone else?
Sign up for my new book alert http://www.
sylviamcdaniel.com/sign-up-for-my-newsletter/ and
receive a complimentary book.**

USA Today Best-selling author, Sylvia McDaniel obviously has too much time on her hands. With over seventy western historical and contemporary romance novels, she spends most days torturing her characters. Bad boys deserve punishment and even good girls get into trouble. Always looking for the next plot twist, she's known for her sweet, funny, family-oriented romances.

Married to her best friend for over twenty-five years, they recently moved to the state of Colorado where they like to hike, and enjoy the beauty of the forest behind their home with their spoiled dachshund Zeus and puppy Bailey. (He has his own column in her newsletter.)

Their grown son, still lives in Texas. An avid football watcher, she loves the Broncos and the Cowboys, especially when they're winning.

www.SylviaMcDaniel.com
Sylvia@SylviaMcDaniel.com
The End!